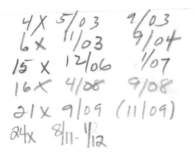

4X 5/03   9/03
6X 11/03   9/04
15 X 12/06   1/07
16X 4/08   9/08
21x 9/09 (11/09)
24x 8/11- 4/12

D0040878

PURE SUNSHINE

GO THERE.

OTHER TITLES AVAILABLE FROM PUSH

Cut
PATRICIA McCORMICK

Kerosene
CHRIS WOODING

You Remind Me of You
EIREANN CORRIGAN

PURE SUNSHINE

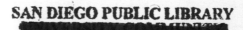

BRIAN JAMES

SCHOLASTIC INC.

NEW YORK   TORONTO   LONDON   AUCKLAND   SYDNEY

MEXICO CITY   NEW DELHI   HONG KONG   BUENOS AIRES

ISBN 0-439-27989-5

12 11 10 9 8 7 6 5 4 3 2 1   2 3 4 5 6 7/0

Printed in the U.S.A.   40
First Scholastic printing, February 2002

This book is dedicated to
Chris and the other Chris,
Ryan, Jamie, Laura, and Sarah-Maria.

Keep on keeping on!

ACKNOWLEDGMENTS

Dan — it is what it is, though
Carrie — someone I've always known
W. Axl Rose — rock ☆ extraordinaire
David — for making scribbles into words
Mom & Dad — thanks for everything

THE SUN FELL FROM THE SKY to go and sleep elsewhere. It was a surrender of sorts, a passing of its reign for the moon to awake. And I lived for that in-between transience when the glass buildings reflected the brilliance of twilight, when the sky was swept with a short and sudden color of flames before fading dull and gray. I waited. On the park bench, I faced the clouds and waited for that perfect moment when the drugs take over.

The shadows of the trees stretched farther in an exhale of length. The rays of the sun were failing to reach the eastern horizon. Headlights switched on by the dozens as the automobiles inched up Walnut Street in the rush-hour maze. I began to see it happen, like the instant of impact in a neutron explosion. The entire city was bathed in crowning light, and for a brief second even Philadelphia appeared to have been carved from gold. I extended my tongue, hoping by chance to ingest the miracle of weather. I felt the bitter stinging. Eager for the photographic flash that occurs when night has taken the edge and all color fades. I waited, knowing that if I blinked I'd miss it completely.

Eyelids open . . pushed to the extreme by cold and wind. The nerve centers of my mouth were growing numb. One fleeting image of intensity before the swollen clouds of evening lulled into view. As the brightness receded overhead, I slowly brought my tongue down, letting it settle in my mouth . . allowing the tab of acid to dissolve further before swallowing.

As I sat up, Kevin and Will, who hadn't paid attention to the changes in the sky, seemed to take their first notice of me in some time. Kevin saw the schoolboy smile broaden across my face. He was confused at first, but then he looked into my eyes and knew.

"Don't tell me you *just* ate yours!" he said, all the while aware that I had. He shook his head in mock reproach. "Why you always hold on to it so long? It'll give you the shits that way."

The smile on my face got wider and wider until I

couldn't hold it back any longer. Glancing over at Will, I saw him struggle with the same strain. When our glances met, we lost it. All three of us just starting laughing. It was like that when the three of us got together. We could be just as unworried as children playing on the monkey bars. And it weren't because of the drugs that we were laughing, not yet. In a few hours maybe, once the strychnine found its merry way into the brain and distorted reality. But right then, we laughed just 'cause we were friends.

But still, giving credit where credit be due, the acid was a bit of a happy pill, our moods changed by the simple fact that we knew in three hours' time we'd be mind-racing like a clown at circus speed. Earlier in the day when school let out, Kevin had been in one of his grumpy phases. As a matter of fact, so had me and Will but we don't wear it like he does. It was only Thursday and we all had that *why isn't it Friday?* feeling.

We had drifted up and down South Street for a stay, looking for girls to meet but only spying the usual-type preteen lassies. The kind with lipsticked faces who try acting older than they are. We were seventeen. Men. We needed real women, and the sight of all those immature schoolgirls frustrated us. I think that's what had set us in our mood, in addition to it being only Thursday and not Friday. That's probably how it would have stayed, too, if we hadn't run into Adam.

Adam was one of those club-gangster types with the turned-back felt Kangol hat and jeans hanging off his ass. But he was also a no-hassle dealer. Didn't give you the runaround. Let you pay with no chitchat. By luck he'd just scored a sheet of California acid. "Pure Sunshine" he'd called it because it had little yellow suns illustrated on each tab. It didn't take much convincing to get our money. For five bucks each we'd be fucked up all night, and our Thursday would be like Friday anyway.

"There's no turning back now, boys," I said once the laughter faded. It was the truth, too. I always had the same sensation after eating acid. It was like driving a fast car directly at a brick wall, and once you passed the marker, you could no longer stop in time. Once you swallowed that tiny piece of paper-dipped toxin, you were in for the long haul. Sitting on that bench I knew that I wouldn't be normal-thinking for another eight to ten hours. I always got a small nervous feeling, like the one you get on the first day of kindergarten. It was a gnawing knot of panic that left me thinking, *There's no turning back now, boys!*

Will would always nod his head when I'd say things of

that sort . . like he was an old wise man with a long white beard who couldn't disagree with some profound truth ventured by a child. I liked it when he did that. It let me know that in some unexplainable way we were connected. That imperceptible nod and the seriousness of his face, admiring that I could state his exact sentiments in such a simplistic phrase.

Kevin leaped up from his perch beside me. Staring us clear in the eyes, he also told it exactly as it was. His voice all full of excitement. "Damn straight we ain't turning back. It's gonna be fire-magic in the head alright."

I never could tell if Kevin got the nervous sickness like Will and I got. If he did, he never showed it. In a way this was a good thing. He'd act as the conductor of our fantasy-fueled orchestra, setting the tempo for us to follow. His enthusiasm was quick in ridding my own doubts. Without him, Will and I probably would have spent the entire night on that bench trapped in some paranoid movie of our own creation, unable to participate in the surreality surrounding us. But something about Kevin's attitude always frightened me. It scared me the way he loved drugs without any inhibitions.

"You're right, you're right. Both of you are always right," Will chimed in. Then he stood. He had a way of moving that the eye could miss, mechanical yet with the swiftness of a snake. When he moved like that, it always threw Kevin and me off guard. In the corner of my eye, I caught Kevin's expression directed at me. He'd seen it, too.

"Where're you two going?" I asked, still seated.

"Umm, nowhere. I don't know." Will suddenly realized that he'd stood for no reason.

"Oh, nowhere," I said softly, as if in contemplation. "Then why don't you guys take a seat? You're jumping around like fucking grasshoppers. It's making me nervous."

I smiled again, getting the laugh out of them I'd wanted. But they didn't sit down right away. I could tell that Will and Kevin were fidgety. They'd probably swallowed their hits a good half hour before I had. I wanted to explain to them it's better to wait for the last second of sunshine. *That* was the true meaning of "Pure Sunshine." But they would have thought I was kidding. I had a habit of creating little rituals that had significance to me alone. Sometimes I'd share them, and Kevin and Will would be understanding and even participate, but I knew they never really *believed* like I did. So I kept this one to myself. Maybe I would tell them later, once we were all peaking and they could appreciate the beauty of idiosyncrasy.

Since I had waited and they hadn't, they were a short step in front of me. I could tell by the slow expanse of the pupils in their eyes . . the way they'd been wringing their hands once I'd finally taken my gaze away from the clouds. Now standing up, they shifted from foot to foot. They'd gotten the itch for new scenery, the one sure sign of the dawning of an acid trip.

As confirmation, they both sat for a second, only to stand right back up again. Knowing I wouldn't win this battle, I also stood. We started to walk, walking right out of the park. The street lamps were on and our slow pace was in step with the soft illumination. I felt my stomach knotting up and realized I was also growing just the least bit anxious.

Center City was abuzz with the bustle of adults heading home. But they were in cars and we were on foot. When the sun sank, Philly was our town. It's not a city like New York or L.A. in the movies, where at night it's alive just like noon. No, Philly's different. Once all those cars traveled the highway to home, they didn't come out again. And when the shops closed at nine, it became a skyscrapered ghost town. Only muggers and misfits, and we enjoyed being a little of both.

We headed downtown, across Broad Street and past City Hall. I felt like waving to the statue of Billy Penn way atop. He looked lonely up there, forever pointing toward nothing in particular. But I didn't wave. It didn't seem worth the effort once the light changed and my feet got going again. I took a cigarette from my pocket instead. I'd been lucky enough not to get carded the day before. I was happy to see I still had an almost full pack. Lord knows I'd need it soon. There was some ingredient in acid that just made a person crave cigarettes. Unchecked, I could go through two packs. And I'm not even a real smoker.

Kevin must have smelled the stale smoke, else he heard the crank of the lighter, 'cause his head whipped around at first puff.

"Shit, you got cigarettes? Why didn't you say anything — gimme one?"

I raised my eyebrows, teasing him. "No way! You and I both know I'll need every last one."

"I'll get some later, come on."

"Yeah, right! Who'll buy them for you? Or are you going to steal some of your mom's Virginia Slims? You can forget it."

"Come on!" Now he was pleading.

"Nope."

While we bantered back and forth, Will moved in that motor-snake way of his again, pulling a fresh cigarette from his own pocket and lighting it with a match. I saw him do it and couldn't help but crack a smile. Kevin turned in his direction only to have his annoyance increase tenfold.

"You bastard, you got some, too? Come on, give me one." But Will and I enjoyed this little sport too much. Neither of us responded. Kevin quickly saw where we were going with this. "That's cool! You're both assholes!"

I took my cigarettes out and handed him one. He took it without thanks and asked if I had a light. Will and I started to laugh again, knowing we could play the game all over. But I didn't want to get Kevin in a mood, especially when we would be tripping in a very short while. So I gave him my lighter.

We walked for a couple of blocks, enjoying the autumn air, which somehow always made a cigarette taste better. As a group, we decided it was best to eat soon. Once the effects of the high kicked in, we'd be too much of a mess to enter any restaurant. Not to mention that acid is about the best diet pill in the world. It wouldn't be long before the sight of food in any form would make us all nauseous. So we headed toward the river, down by Chestnut Street where the restaurants were dark.

We chose an uncrowded location. It was probably

fancier than it should have been. With our faded jeans and secondhand thrift store shirts, we didn't exactly fit in. Actually, we stood out like London street punks in a Baptist church down South. Our drugged appearance got the disapproving looks from the few other customers and the hostess alike. We sort of appreciated that, though. It reassured us that we were not like them. <u>We were not nine-to-five Republicans</u>. It was uplifting to create a stir whenever we entered one of those places. An in-your-face gesture, like we had said, "Look, we're gonna change your world and we don't care if you like it or not," just by walking in. Will even had the courage to light another cigarette as the middle-aged hostess showed us to our table, way in the back. God, I fucking loved when he did stuff like that.

We sat down and pulled in our chairs, and I felt a sudden sense of adventure. The night was slipping into insanity, and I was aware of it. There was no turning back now, and I loved it.

SIMPLY PUT, IT WAS A BAD IDEA. We'd have been much better off getting hot dogs at the grease trucks up on Market. I completely forgot to calculate the time spent waiting for service . . the twenty minutes before the unfriendly waiter takes your order, the other forty it takes to actually get your food, and the near half hour you wait once you've eaten before you can get the lousy check. It was always the same in restaurants like that. The service sucked because they knew there was no tip coming from a group of degenerates who looked like we did.

It was just bad planning on our part. We'd figured dinner would be an hour. That would be an hour, an hour and a half since we'd taken our hits. Whenever we took acid, it was like keeping a synchronized clock in our heads. We had to stick to the agenda, time zero equaling the moment we took the tabs. Two hours is the latent period. Two hours is what we had from time zero until the spaceship left from landing.

We had figured on only an hour. Perfect timing. It went to show our judgment was already clouded upon entering. No way an hour in a joint like that looking like we did. By the time the food was slammed down, I could hardly stand the sight of it.

I ate the fries and left three-quarters of my burger to rot. Will and Kevin were worse. They couldn't even touch the fries.

Since there was so much food still on our plates, the dumb-ass waiter never bothered to come back. I swear they run restaurants like a nagging mother would; you can't leave the table until you clear your plate. Fuck that, we wanted to get outta there quick.

The dim light caused a slight spinning effect on the porcelain dishes. My glass of water started to make me dizzy. A tiny piece of food floated on top and I imagined it expanding . . growing tentacles and giving birth to many others of its kind, taking over my drinking water. I shook the image off quicker than I would've had I not been in public. I didn't want the visuals yet. Not until I was out in the open air and could breathe again. I was already getting the lockjaw side effect.

Kevin was on the verge. He'd already spit water through his nose in a fit of uncontrollable laughter. That had set off a chain reaction of silly behavior. Will dropped his napkin from his lap, bent to pick it up, taking his silverware and nearly his whole dinner with him. It was coming like a tidal wave. Had to be careful not to roll out of there on the floor.

"Alright, serious now. We gotta get a grip," I said, containing my own spasms. For a brief second, we achieved an acceptable silence. But that went as quick as it had come. No choice now. Since I was the one with the most sense left, I flagged down the waiter. Told him we needed to go and asked in a false politeness if we could kindly get our check. When he came back, Will held his money out and dropped it on the floor in front of the waiter. Kevin went head down, it was just too much. Making an about-face, our annoyed waiter took his leave from our night. We left exact change on the table and made our escape.

We emerged from that candlelit extravagance like nuclear holocaust survivors from their backyard bomb shelters. The pupils of our eyes were in full eclipse. I could hear the screams in my head again. All my make-believe friends had returned.

The travels of pedestrians and the steady honking of traffic had thrown us into momentary confusion. We stood on the corner like drifters in a time slip. Though we'd lived in the city all our lives, we were temporarily impaired. Nothing looked right. But everything looked vaguely familiar at the same time.

"Ohhhhhhh, shiiit," Will said, staring up at a street sign as if it were written in alien calligraphy. "I'm a wreck," he added with the smile that was slowly becoming a permanent fixture on his face.

"You got that right!" Kevin said this while attempting to pickpocket Will's cigarettes. Will slapped his hand away, only to give him one anyway.

I fixed my gaze on the approaching headlights. I was mesmerized by the geometry of reflection as the light bounced from one chrome-painted finish to the next. I felt like a four-year-old at a fireworks display. This was definitely some good acid. Usually these little exhibitions of the commonplace didn't affect me unless I was at my chemical peak. I had expected a slight blurring effect, but this was the real deal.

"It's yellow," I said, already able to tell.

"What is?"

I turned toward Kevin, trying hard to concentrate on his face as it moved in slow distortions. "Everything's yellow! See, over there." I pointed to the tall buildings uptown, windows lit by overtime employees. "The acid. It's lemon-flavored."

Will nodded in that way of his again. Every batch of acid has particular qualities. Some are more auditory than visual. Others are better suited for snow than sunshine. You might call those a kind of winter brew, like they do with beer. Some create a more greenish hue on the objects around; others are yellow like the hits we'd just taken. Will and I considered ourselves connoisseurs, like wine tasters at a convention. We always made a point of identifying what kind we had as soon as we noticed.

He examined the buildings, the people passing by, and even his own hands before approving my assessment. Of course, it's impossible to disagree with the first hypothesis presented. Once a specific color is suggested, that's all the eye begins to look for.

I could see from his agitated movements that Kevin was growing restless. The drug has a way of doing that. You have to keep moving . . keep changing the setting.

It's like a pain you have to walk off. Keep still and it gets too intense, lifts itself up along the spine until your head falls into a tailspin.

"Come on, where we going? I can't stand here any longer!"

"I don't know?" I answered, highlighting the second lapse of judgment in our still-young night. We never really had a plan. It's best to have a plan. Gotta have a place to be when the jets kick in. We were approaching full gear with nowhere to go. I was also feeling that need. The need for a safe house, for home base. I'd be damned if I was gonna spend my entire trip on the streets. That's the sure way to lose your mind.

Will shrugged his shoulders. "We could go to Sally's. She lives right around here."

Sally was this girl two years behind us in school. None of us really cared too much for her. She was no scholar, which is a nice way of saying she was as stupid as a cat's ass. Still she was kinda cute in a girlish way . . too clumsy to be sexy but a real pretty face and a tight body.

She worshiped the three of us. Thought everything we said was so damn cool. We could make her bust a gut laughing one minute and have her mind grow into vacant confusion the next. She never knew what we were going to do. In many ways, I think she was scared out of her mind by us . . or at least intimidated as hell. That's why we hung with her. She thought we were regular geniuses, and so did we.

We didn't need to impress her. Least, I didn't because I couldn't give a fuck what she'd get going on in her head about me. Sure, she was a girl, so sex was spinning around in my brain. But she was a wasted effort in a way. Too young to be serious and not really who I dreamed about. I had my heart set somewhere else. But I didn't fuss over it, I wasn't in any state to try to impress so it didn't really matter which girl we went to see. Matter of fact, it's probably better that we were heading for Sally's and not someone's I actually gave a shit about.

Sally lived about ten blocks from that wasteland of a restaurant. Down in the river section of Society Hill, where tourists still came to see where old Ben Franklin had lived. Old-money district.

My, Kevin's, and Will's spirits were on the rise now that we had gathered our wits and come up with what was almost a plan.

We had been trying to trip up one another for two blocks, trying to see who'd be the first to fall flat on his face. Cutting into the other's path with a sidestep swagger, hoping the other person wouldn't catch himself in time. This ain't an easy task when your blood is burning up hallucinogens at the rate a beat-up, old 70s Plymouth guzzles gasoline. It never worked, though. The only time anyone fell was when he'd lost his own balance trying to get into position. It was still fun. We had a laugh with it. But we also burned down from it. Couldn't even make it the ten blocks without needing to sit in order to catch our wind.

I smoked another cigarette. It was already starting. I felt the chain-smoker mentality coming with a vengeance. But fuck it. I knew I wouldn't be able to smoke in Sally's prissy house. She was a clean-cut girl, the kind that would occasionally still wear a dress. I had a deep and sudden wish that when we did get there, she'd open the door wearing one. Probably, she wouldn't even know we were fucked up . .

Just for sport, Kevin had taken to asking passersby for spare change. Every time he did, Will would start giggling. Soon they were creating such a spectacle that I, too, took to giggling. I couldn't help it. The people's faces all resembled misfired animation projects . . rejected toons from a twisted children's show.

Kevin went right on asking. Speaking louder than he

needed to, almost shouting at everyone who by some stroke of bad luck ended up walking past us. They all turned their noses up sourly . . scrunching their faces in the most ridiculous expressions. Will and I exploded right in their snobby faces, exaggerating the volume of our laughter for their irritation.

"GOT SOME CHANGE? GOT SOME CHANGE?" Kevin's voice was swimming in my head. He had fallen into the broken record syndrome. It happened now and then. Once you started repeating something like that, again and again, the acid sort of got stuck on it. Kevin had no more control over it than an ant does on the tides. His voice kept booming up and down the street. "GOT SOME CHANGE? GOT SOME CHANGE?"

He really needed some, too! Like an infant with a craving, he'd whine and moan until someone gave in.

The next person to come down the block was a young mother pushing a stroller. I knew right off this was bad news. Kevin was ready to snap. She had definitely heard him from way down, which'd given her plenty of paces to get agitated. I felt my muscles as they got tense. It was gonna be the show of shows very soon.

As soon as they got into clear sight, I lost it. The baby's head looked HUGE. It seemed to take up my entire vision. For a brief moment I thought maybe it wasn't even real. It was like a helium cartoon with live-action goo-goo noises. They got within a few yards before I pointed at the little tyke, calling out in a stereotyped Italian accent, "ITSZA BABEEE!" This had been a standard with us, no matter what the drug. When babies went by in strollers, we treated it like a cosmic event. Something to do with the way their tiny faces twitched under the observation of a narcotic stare. None of us really knew why it was funny, but it had been once, and through routine it had developed into one of our classic inside jokes. It always knocked the parents out of the box. (This poor woman was no exception.) They never expected it, and their surprise is what I think we loved most about the whole thing.

The young mother was just near done looking me over when Kevin sprung at her, startling her out of her wits. I thought I saw her arms flail like a stung bird, but it could've been my unsound imagination. "GOT SOME CHANGE?" he roared at her, and I pictured the wind of his words knocking her back on her ass.

One good look into our eyes and the woman knew we weren't all there. She felt confident enough in her class status to brush us off, drugged or undrugged. I half heard her saying, "Why don't you get a job," or something of that type. I lost interest in her. Will and I were busy making all kinds of silly faces to amuse the baby, who was taking immense pleasure in our antics.

"Why I need a job if you just GIVE ME SOME CHANGE!" Kevin was in rare form. She wheeled around him and continued down the street. I saw the break in Kevin's face. The record needle had advanced and he could move on. As the woman walked off, we saw the little baby leaning over, looking back. And with a smile, the little tyke actually waved to us. We waved back and chalked it up as a victory. We'd taught that little kid how to live a little.

We took off running, a bit afraid that maybe that woman would tell the first police officer she saw that a couple of doped-up kids were harassing good people. We were in no condition to deal with that shit. Had to keep on moving. Had to get to Sally's and set up camp before it was too late.

We stood in front of Sally's door. It was nine-thirty, ten o'clock. A good two hours since we'd decided to go there. It took a lot longer than we'd anticipated to regain composure after our little run-in with the amusement train. Those five blocks were expanded in our unbalanced state of mind. We'd run off in the completely wrong direction, then got sidetracked by a colorful window display advertising the far-off Christmas season. But we'd made it. A little late, granted, but we had certainly made it.

Sally's house was dark, and we were daring one another to knock on the heavy wooden door. None of us wanted to be the one to greet the angry face of her mom or pops. Will suggested we just climb through the window and break in. He was only half joking. I volunteered Kevin for the job. Will seconded the motion, but Kevin definitely wasn't flattered by the gesture.

"You fucking do it, it was your idea to come here in the first place," he said to Will. Will and I started laughing again because we could tell Kevin was getting the frustration inside him. It was cold outside, and he really just wanted somewhere besides the cement sidewalk to sit on.

"Or Brendon, you do it. Her mom likes you."

It was true, her mom did sort of like me, 'cause I was the only one of us heathens that had any manners. But I was in no condition to deal with Sally's rich, dignified mother at this juncture.

"Nope," was all I said. Then I thought about it and added, "Well, alright. If you give me a cigarette, I'll do it."

"Fuck you, you know I don't have any. Come on, just do it. It's freezing out here!"

Will and I shouldn't have tormented Kevin like this, but it really was fun to watch him pout. We could afford to bluff in this way because we knew, no matter what, there was no way in hell Kevin was gonna knock on that door. And he knew it, too. He treated any activity involving adults and their formalities like a terminal disease to be avoided at all costs. That's why he would've pleaded with us for hours to get one of us to put fist to wood and gain our unsightly selves access to that relative palace. That is, if Sally hadn't heard us and looked down from her third-floor bedroom window.

"Hey, what are you guys doing down there? Why didn't you knock like normal people instead making all that noise?" We couldn't help but laugh when she said that, thus creating more noise that she didn't want. "Shhhh! I'm coming down. And Brendon, put that cigarette out, my parents will kill me if they smell smoke on you guys."

We saw her little head bob back into the house. I had just lit that cigarette and would be damned if I was gonna put it out before I was at least halfway down to the filter. We could hear her padded steps trooping down the stairs toward us. Kevin was already relieved. We all looked at one another like parachuters readying themselves to take the plunge from the airplane. "OK, boys, behave yourselves," Will added as precaution as Sally's slender hand turned the knob from the other side.

She pulled the door back, her pretty face wrung tight in a genuine smile. I threw my cigarette down and stomped it out to make Smokey proud. Her eyes were lit up, 'cause her admiration for us was truly out of this world.

She beckoned us to take off our boots in the foyer. It was lit by a low-hanging chandelier crafted from fine crystal. The three of us were trying hard not to lose it. I had the sudden sense that we had walked into an after-hours museum. There was that unnerving quiet about Sally's house all the time. There was no way we would be able to follow the rules. We were falling about just trying to take our shoes off our feet. But I knew once we got up the three flights of stairs, we could let loose. It was just enough to keep me sane. I was gonna make it.

Then Sally's high-pitched scream echoed in my ear. "It's just the guys, Mom! Will and Brendon and Kevin. We're going upstairs for a little bit!"

"What the hell did you scream in my ear for? I didn't even hear her ask nothing! Jesus Christ!" I said, secretly noting how she referred to us as "the guys." We were just about the only male friends Sally had, her being too prissy and all for anyone to really hang out with her.

"Sorry," she whispered, and even in my cloudy judgment I could tell she was sincere. We had been knocking around like The Three Stooges but had finally succeeded in getting our boots off without breaking anything. "Come on, you guys, let's go upstairs."

She wasn't wearing a dress, but she did have a skirt on. Will and I shoved each other for position in order to be the one who got to look up it as we scaled the flights of seemingly endless steps. He won and turned around to give me a smirk to let me know it.

The three of us were already laughing like grade-school boys by the time we'd reached the second floor. On the way to the third, Kevin missed a step and fell, barely catching himself with his hands. Too late, we'd lost it. But it was like the elements were conspiring against us. We'd really tried hard. Kevin stood too quickly for his sight to handle, and we all raced at top speed through Sally's bedroom door, slamming it behind us.

Sally gave us that smug little look of approval. I could

tell our presence had livened up her dull evening. I was also aware that it was getting harder and harder to focus on anything. The ceiling and the floor had taken to spinning in opposite directions. And her room was filled with girlish decorations of every sort. It was an affront to my magnified senses .. splatterings of pink and white everywhere like doll vomit. Even under normal circumstance, her room never settled right in the pit of my stomach.

"What are you, blind?" Will announced, and I could tell he was just as put off by the brightness of the room as I was.

"What?" Sally asked, having no idea whatsoever what Will was referring to.

"You got practically every light in the world on in here."

Sally said something like "oh," and went around turning each one off until there was only the one lamp on, atop the nightstand beside her bed. Her room was huge. It was the whole floor of a converted attic. Besides the canopy bed, dresser, and other usual furnishings, Sally had a sectional sofa equipped with an accompanying coffee table. That's where Will and I took refuge while Kevin made a beeline for the bed. Leaping with two-footed agility, he plopped facedown, burying his swirling head in the satin pillow sheets.

Sally waltzed over to me and Will in a prancing sort of way. Christ, she was such a sophomore. She was definitely enjoying the attention as much as we were enjoying the comfort of four walls, a ceiling, and a floor. "You wanna listen to music?" she asked. We nodded unenthusiastically, since we knew she only had crap.

She put on some pop album she'd recently purchased and took a seat between me and Will. It was the first music we'd heard since we'd starting tripping. It sounded strange and faraway, like it was coming from downstairs. But still the notes got into my head. It was infectious. The quirky beats and the singer's bubblegum voice exploded. In a fantasy, I saw hundreds of little gnomes dancing around to the beat. They were locking arms, doing the swing-your-partner routine. I could see the whole magic land they inhabited. And I knew I'd probably go out and buy that horrible album the next day.

We bullshitted for a while on her couch, keeping as coherent as we were capable of doing. We made fun of every nobody we knew in school, teachers included. Sally was hurting from laughing so hard. She didn't try to make her own jokes — too insecure around us. Her cropped, curly hair was shaking with the motions of her chest. She really was a pretty girl.

Kevin hadn't moved from his frozen place on the bed.

Head buried farther and farther in the pillows, he was flying through some dream vision .. exploring the many tunnels that the acid had opened for him. Best to let him lie, even though I was missing his company.

Will leaned over and kissed Sally square on the mouth. God, the courage he had. Certainly we had fooled around with her before, but man, to just lean over and kiss her without any leading up to it. It just killed me the way he did things sometimes. I could see the Romeo streak taking light in his wildfire eyes.

Sally responded in the positive. She leaned over to return his kiss, but he stopped her, saying, "Kiss Brendon, don't kiss me." She looked at him uneasily. Then she smiled. She looked to me. I tried not to look too closely. Whenever you trip, people's faces don't look quite real. It's like they got rubber masks of their own faces on. Still, I wasn't about to stop her from kissing me.

She did. Closed like the one Will had given her. I jammed my tongue in her mouth as she pressed her lips to mine. I kept my eyes shut tight so I wouldn't have to see her expression, which was probably welcoming even if it was startled. It was the first time I'd really closed my eyes tight since I'd taken my hit. I had almost forgotten that when you close your eyes, you're immediately transported to some foreign dimension, and any hold on the reality beyond the closed eyelids is momentarily lost. I quickly opened them again, afraid of what I'd seen when they were shut, glad to see Sally's close-range face even if the acid did magnify every pore on it.

"Let's play Jesus," Will offered. Sally smiled, though I knew she had no fucking idea what the hell he was talking about. I knew because I myself had no idea what he was going to say next. He had his way of pulling the craziest shit from out of God knows where and flinging it in your face like you should know from the get-go what he was talking about.

"You know! Let's play Jesus. You're the Virgin Mary, and Brendon and me, and maybe Kevin if he ever gets up . . we're the Three Wise Men. You take off your clothes, and we look to see if there's a baby coming."

I started laughing right off. Sally joined me, but I could tell there was nervousness in it. She wasn't sure if he was kidding or not. I knew he was kidding, but if she would agree, he'd be more than serious. She liked Will and me and all, but Kevin kinda frightened her. And being as though we'd just heard the first peep out of him in some time when he heard Will's comment, it didn't help to ease her any.

She never did take off her clothes, not that I ever expected her to. In this quivering tone she told us that there was no way, and I thought maybe the whole fooling-around thing would be called off, but both Will and I did manage to steal a little more attention from her before she had to show us out at her mom's request. Sally had to straighten herself up when Mom came banging on the door. Her hair was disheveled and she had a guilty look on her face. Will and I sat there, our faces stuck in that lockjaw smile. Kevin was still half passed-out on the bed. Sally's mom stepped into the room, and true to form, I was the only one who said hello. She gave us that smile, the one that says, "Nice to see you. Have you misfits been fondling my daughter again?" She told Sally it was getting late and her friends had to go now. It cracked me up how wholesome they were. The way she couldn't come in like my mom and say, "What the hell are your friends still doing here? Tell them to get out before I throw them out."

We took our cue. After Sally's mom retreated back into the walls from which she came, Will and I went over and shook Kevin out of his paranoid coma. He had spent the whole time he was peaking facedown, drooling on Sally's bed. I shook my head, not knowing how he could handle that kind of nightmare.

IT WAS JUST AROUND MIDNIGHT when Sally locked the door behind us. Luckily I had phoned my mom earlier and told her I would be staying at Kevin's. My brain was fried. The cycle was spinning down to the tail end. We'd given Sally plenty of stories to go bragging to her fifteen-year-old girlfriends about . . the old "guess who? guess what?" and all that. I was sure I'd hear about some of the things I'd forgotten. Gossip could be good that way. Sometimes it helps you learn your own secrets.

We lit about five cigarettes each. Smoked 'em one after the other. I was getting the shakes pretty bad. That was from my system running down, working the poison out of my body in slow motion. I knew there'd still be the occasional kick start, though. The acid would inch back up even after it had faded from peak. We were all still pretty fucked up and it was still steady. But as the night made its way into early morning, it had taken on an edge.

We cut over and crossed by the Liberty Bell. We pressed our faces to the bulletproof glass protecting it. Part of me wanted to kick that glass in and ring on that bell until it shattered, until the people sleeping in their beds out in Jersey could hear it. But that was an impossible dream because the bell's off-limits. It's like they were already planning for the time when it would be dug up like the Colosseum. Our breath fogged up the glass until ole Liberty frosted out of view and disappeared. It wasn't worth the effort to wipe the glass, so I turned away.

Alone, I went over to the center of the park and stared across the street at Independence Hall. If I squinted my eyes, it looked a little like a model. The air was cold and gave every object a strange icy halo. I raised my featherless arms to my sides. I wanted to change the constitution of nature and take to the sky on ashen wings. I'd fly to the tower and back two hundred or so years. I'd watch the cannons being wheeled along the cobbled streets by men in red wool coats. Bricks would fly as ammunition struck them, and I would remain abstracted above it all.

And when the war had ended and there was nothing more for me to see, I'd fly even farther away . . bull's-eye through the counterclockwise cloud spins on my way to the distant stars.

Under the alterations of LSD, this dream felt near, or at least for a few brief and happy seconds it did. It was never-lasting.

Will and Kevin came sauntering quickly across the park, capturing my attention away. They were moving real quiet but they were also moving real quick. "There you are . . we thought we lost you," Will said, laughing. "We didn't know where you went. Man, I thought you just went to take a piss."

I could tell they'd probably looked behind every bush for me. Their faces were hiding a secret. I could see mischief written across their expressions. They looked like little kids who'd just found a porno mag in the woods.

"What've you got?" I asked.

Will was rubbing his hands. He spoke in a singsong tone when saying, "Nothing . . *but Kevin's gotta joint.*"

I think we literally jumped and danced, hollering at the top of our lungs. We had deteriorated into a roving madcap gang when Kevin produced the perfectly rolled paper from behind his back. It was as if our strung-out senses couldn't handle this kind of temporal overload. My trip had been getting too reflective for my own tastes. A little weed was just the boost I needed.

It only felt right that this journey toward freedom of consciousness should start where it did. Right on the site of the Revolution. Man, sometimes I get a real kick out of history. It's like all these loose blocks just sitting around for you to pick 'em up and make what you want from them. When Kevin sparked the flame of my lighter, I watched the way the joint burned, and I felt that somehow we were all connected to it through the smoke it gave off.

We passed the joint in step as we headed off into Old City, the fifteen or so crammed blocks down by the waterfront. On a whim, Will had taken to goose-stepping. The soles of his heavy boots clanked down hard against the stones. The sound echoed wildly through the empty tunnel of streets. From streetlight to streetlight, our shadows went through alterations of growth and decline. Will's lengthening shadow would make the most obscene sight as he marched in that spindle-legged way. Through the clouds of smoke that we released, the whole scene took on an eerie horror quality.

Kevin kept making these weak-throated roars, attempting to soundtrack the event. Anyone listening from their apartments would have thought a couple of criminal lunatics had been set free. I started imagining the different kinds of creatures that would be lurking around the next corner. I took to whispering their descriptions to Will and Kevin . . "a sawed-off troll with plaster shoes . . a mutilated ape gnawing on aborted limbs," and such, so forth, and so on. We were really working the rhythm of it. So much so that I was getting far too bugged out. I was buying hard into my own fictions.

I had to call off the whole show and find a seat leaning against a closed shop window. Best to stop the production before it got too real and too late to shake. I needed to chill for a minute. The marijuana had gone to the head like a rocket on account of my toxin-washed veins. I had developed a minor case of drying sickness. My hands involuntarily caught up in muscular contractions. The influx of various narcotics within my body produced a glorious numbing effect on all the nerve centers. And everything around me had a glazed appearance.

Will took his place at my side, fitting himself onto the

cold cement. I looked over at him but had to turn away. His face was turning around in circular shades of green-ish gradations. I felt my spirit drifting off on some nomadic quest, and every time I grasped to reel it back in, it only roamed further.

I wasn't even conscious of speaking aloud, but I was saying, "Whoa horsies, Whoooaa Hoorsies!" over and over. Will was in a fit beside me. This was our little phrase . . our personal mantra for when a high had got-ten a little too crazy.

Kevin looked down at the two of us sitting on the ground. He looked us dead in the eye. How he was able to keep a straight face was beyond me, knowing what he was going to say next. But he had his way. He took one last toke on the joint before it burned his fingers and then looked at us flat, his stance taken from an old 50s movie. I was trapped in a chorus of "whooaa horsies" when he hit us with "little Lex Luthor on a pony." Man, he could be so suave sometimes. I mean, to just shoot shit from the hip like that and say it like he meant busi-ness, like it was the most important piece of information that we were missing.

Will was in contortions by then. Carried away with excitement, he called out at the top of his lungs, "Caught your mom, who bought it from the grocery!"

This set off a chain reaction of nonsense quotations. We took to chanting the whole bit to some imagined meter: *"Whoa Horsies, Whooa Hoorsies! Little Lex Luthor on a pony, caught your mom who bought it from the grocery."* We went through nearly twenty verses. Singing at full volume, sounding like drunken sailors on leave.

That was about the last true storm of acid that night. When we'd exhausted the pleasure from the song, we'd used up the reserves. Oh, the residuals were still there alright. We didn't have any clearheadedness. We could still feel the tingling in the spine and the tiny distortion in vision. But the moment had passed, and we were running full speed down the spiral. It was a relief in many ways. It was always like that, good to be back on the ambulance to feeling well.

Kevin's house was just south of the bridge. We wandered for some time around Old City before going back there. We wanted to make sure we completely walked it off just in case Kevin's mom or dad was waiting up for us. It wasn't likely, but it's always better to be a little later for safety's sake.

It was just after three in the morning when we arrived. Rise-and-shine was only four hours away due to it being a school night and all. We were tired, but in no way was sleep in the forecast. It's near impossible to sleep after you've tripped. Soon as you close your eyes the drug builds momentum all over again.

We went through the motions of going to bed. You could hear the late-night cars traveling back and forth. Their high-pitched hum made it difficult to concentrate on sleep. I washed the sweat from my face and urinated for five straight minutes. I was flushing the evil out. It finds exit through the pores and the bladder. It was a good feeling knowing even though I might not be able to sleep, at least I'd feel clean.

Will and I took blankets from the hall closet and threw them into a makeshift bed on the floor. While Kevin was in the bathroom doing his nighttime routine, we stole the pillows, off his bed, figuring he already had the bed, so why should he get all the nice soft pillows, too? Surprisingly, he didn't put up much of a fight when he got back. I guess he saw the logic of the situation.

The three of us lay there in the dark and talked about the different ways we'd commit suicide if the urge ever struck us. It's not like we were infatuated with death or that we were depressed in any unusual way. It was just that the prospect of living a long life seemed like such a chore. Just so damned bored with everything! When I was younger, I remembered seeing a band logo that read, "Live Like a Suicide!" And I guess that's sort of how we felt . . young and reckless because nothing ever mattered in the grand scheme of things anyway.

Will had just finished telling us how he would go with a gun to his head. *Boom!* Erased in an instant blast of glory. His thinking was that if you were determined to go all the way, might as well go and do it right. Send the brain out the side on the express train. Snuff it all in a little spark of powder and a twitch of the finger.

I could never have done it that way. The image of human tissue infected with metal was too much for me to stomach. No, I would plug the exhaust pipe of an automobile and keep it running in a closed garage letting the carbon monoxide wash over me and lull me to sleep. I explained to them my belief that, in death, the soul lived forever in the last living thought. My way, you could die painless as you slept. You could even have music on to set the mood. My way would mean dying happy. With a bullet, the last thought is inevitably fear and pain. I told Will I knew I didn't want my soul living forever caught up in that baggage. He nodded in his way, but it wasn't in agreement. It was out of sympathy and acceptance of ideas. That was enough for me and I let it lie.

Kevin didn't participate. He'd wrapped the covers over his head. I doubt he was actually asleep, but there was no need to press. The sun was somewhere just below the horizon. I closed my eyes and struggled with the internal visions. Patterns emerged in every direction and I shook them off in turn. I could hear the continuous motor hum of cars driving from state to state across the bridge. And for the first time I realized that it was now Friday.

I tossed and turned, trying to relieve my cramped legs and stiff back. I ignored the cold sweats and sleepless anxiety that crept up. I rocked back and forth like a baby or a trauma victim, saying over and over in my head that famous line, "Hurry up, please, it's time. Hurry up, please, it's time." The bar was closing down. Last call. No more waiting for a table. No more stalled engines. My mind was free to go where it would . . released from all chemical authority. It was the old 'bye for now, catch you again some other day. I had nothing left to give. I gave up all resistance, but somewhere deep down there was a stirring calm that assured me that all was going to be okay.

BY THE TIME THIRD PERIOD HAD STARTED, I was like the walking dead. My eyelids drooped like rocks were tied to 'em. Heavy outlines circled 'em, and I looked like shit. Kevin hadn't had any clean clothes for us to wear because he never bothered doing laundry, and there was no way I was going to put on any of his grimy clothes. Will and I just switched our own shirts, but even that wasn't much better. We'd sweated through those in the previous night's reflux, so instead of my smell I had his. And smell I did, but I consoled myself with the fact that certain chicks dug that shit. Or at least that's how I tried to console myself.

When I woke up in the morning it was the first I was

aware that I'd ever fallen asleep to begin with. It goes like that sometimes, you never know you've slept until you're damn sure you woke up. I felt like I'd been run over by a truck. My whole body ached and my stomach was screaming for food. But when I saw myself in the bathroom mirror, my whole appetite went the way of the water in the drain. My first clear thought was, *Well, I survived another one.*

As I sat in class, I wasn't able to keep focus. I was barely hearing the teacher ramble on about this and that, something or other to do with diseases spreading through Southeast Asia. On any other day it might have been fascinating, but on no sleep it was just noise. Noise and the stupid need for attendance. I had thought hard on cutting, but my mom always checked up on the days I'd spent out, just to make sure I was keeping my promises.

Kevin had fought with his mother that morning about what time we got in. He said around one, which was a lie, and she called it a lie, too. She'd still been up then. Truth was, Kevin just wasn't sure what time it was when we'd gotten there. But he sure as shit knew it weren't no one o'clock. And like I said, so did his mom, and she called a spade a spade. But it wasn't like she got real mad. She gave one of those parental looks of disapproval and left it at that. I was just always amazed that we could stay out that late anyway. My house, it was eleven on a school night. That's why my mom checked up. She knew that I stayed out in order to stay out. And that's also why I hadn't cut because I wanted the policy to continue that way.

The first two periods had been real tough. First period I had gym class, which was a cruelty in its own right. No sooner had I put the last of my effort into getting dressed and getting to school on time than I had to go through the reverse all over again. Not that I ever participated in gym activities anyway, but still I had to go through the motions of putting on even dirtier clothes.

We had played some twisted form of dodgeball that the instructor thought up. The jocks had been real into it. They were chucking foam balls from one end of the auditorium to the other at full velocity. I got hit hard in the head within the first ten minutes. I sat on the side the rest of the period. I think I even nodded off for a stretch because when it was time to go back into the locker room, the teacher came over and informed me that I'd lose credit for the day. Oh yeah that hurt me! Fuck him, anyway. Everyone knew no college gave a rat's ass what your phys ed transcript looked like.

Second period had been somewhat of a mixed bag. It was my world history class, which I usually enjoyed, but it started on the wrong foot from the moment the bell announced its beginning. We'd been assigned a one-page essay to be handed in that day. Naturally I hadn't got around to writing it the night before, being busy with other, more ethereal things. The teacher hadn't taken too kindly to my secondhand excuse. I was a good student, really. She didn't appreciate it when good students blew off assignments. I was too tired to honestly feel bad about it, though.

Since the teacher had soured on me, I took myself out of the class discussions for the day. I didn't really have much to say, regardless. But like I said, it was a mixed bag, because second period was the first class of the day that I had with Melissa.

Melissa was that adorable type of girl. Intelligent and quick. She stood out from the rest. A tiger in a desert. A bird hovering above the sewage. The kind of girl who is so attractive by the simple fact that she has no idea she is attractive. She had the kind of strawberry-color hair a guy could go nuts staring at all the time. That's what I did. I went nuts staring at her all the time.

She was the one haunting my thoughts in those moments before sleep. Filmstrip dreams of us in the sunset of some foreign scene. Faded photographs of a future with me and the life we lead. She was the one of fantasy, of make-believe, and I felt so damn stupid for all the dull things I said to her when I spoke.

Even though at times I thought the extent of my crush was incredibly obvious, I didn't think she really had any idea. I sat a few seats behind her and spent the whole class mesmerized by the way her hair clung lightly to the back of her neck. God, how I wanted to just stand up, walk over, and place the palm of my hand there and whisper to her that I loved her. But for better or for worse, that just ain't the way it's done, and whatever the right way was, I was completely in the dark.

My friend Ryan had dated her the year before. Ryan was about the nicest guy in the world when it came to friends. But when you were dealing in boyfriends, he could be subpar. Not to say he was abusive or that he cheated or anything like that. It's just he could be oblivious to things that were hurting.

It had been that way with Melissa and him. I think he really cared for her, but they just weren't a match. I had been friends with both of them during the ordeal and even before, so it was hard seeing one friend upsetting the other so much.

Usually when that type of mess happens, I try to stay on neutral ground. But when the shit was going to hell between Ryan and her, it had been different. They always bickered and he picked on her and all the rest. It was impossible for me not to take sides.

Melissa would always come over to my house, her eyes pink and swollen with tears. I'd listen. Sometimes we'd talk straight through until morning about all sorts of things. We had so much in common . . so many of the important things that mattered.

She would lie on my bed, sobbing beautifully. Fighting through tears once, she told me how she and Ryan fought because she wasn't ready for sex yet. "Not that I'm a goddamn saint and won't ever! I just want it to be special . . to be in love, that's all," she confided.

That was the first time I opened up to her. I told her that I was also a virgin-in-waiting . . saving it for someone perfect. Kevin and Will were the only ones I'd ever admitted it to before. A guy has to keep that kind of truth a secret . . too much pressure . . macho-ness and all that hateful stuff. It was taboo to tell a girl something like that, especially one who knew the people you did. Lies get exposed that way. But Melissa was upset. Ryan had made her think she was some type of mutant. I couldn't bear to have her believing *that*.

When I told her "me, too," she acted surprised. It wasn't the knowledge that caught her off guard, it was the fact that I told her. She was moved that I felt I could trust her. There was an instant connection. We'd each found someone else who held tight to leftover romanticism. It opened doors for us to share all our fears and our dreams. She would speak about wanting children and how she was afraid of growing old and poor. And I'd listen . . her voice like water as I kissed it into me.

During those months, I saw beneath the makeup and the pretenses and got to know her for who she really was. She wasn't selfish about it. She also asked me about me and not about what Ryan or anyone else might have said about her. I'd tell her how I didn't want to live past forty and she'd laugh, not because it was funny but because she thought the same.

There was nothing fake about her. She didn't fly from scene to scene trying to stay up on the world of what is hip and fashionable. She wasn't like those party girls with mad style and nothing much happening up in the head. Melissa had the world figured out — she just chose not to participate in its chaos.

We were really close then, but it didn't last.

She had waited for me to say something for a long time, to tell her I didn't want her to ever go away. But I waited too long, I suppose, because by the time I felt ready, she was already telling me about some great new somebody else she had met. I could've told her then, and maybe she would've chosen me. But I didn't. I kept my love shut up. I faked enthusiasm as I watched her end up with someone else. I was left with just another acquaintance when I'd thought I'd found someone special.

I wasn't ready to give it all up. The fancy phrases. The uppers. The downers. The cages. Pretensions and persuasions. I loved the world of fantasies and miracles and flashy lights in dark spaces. With Melissa, I was only myself. I couldn't play the parts. Couldn't believe my own lies. With her, everything was so real . . so sober. It fucking well scared the piss out of me.

Thinking about it all and staring at the curve of her posture, I wanted to go up to her after class and ask her out for the night or for the next night or the next week for that matter. I just wanted to spend whatever time I could alone with her . . alone to look closely at her speckled green eyes. To tell her what an ass I had been and that I wanted to be rooted to her world if she'd welcome me. She had since broken it off with that other guy, and I didn't want to miss another opportunity.

For whatever reason I didn't ask her, though. "Too tired," I told myself, but in truth I was too scared of rejection. My inaction at the end of class was part of the reason why third period was worse than it should've been.

Halfway through our lecture on the death of Asia, I had looked around and noticed three or four other students with their heads down or just plain flopping back with their mouths open. It was reassuring to know that the teacher was boring the others to the same extent he was boring me. He was on his last year before retiring and had given up a long time ago. He read straight from the lesson plans he'd written twenty, thirty years ago. No reason to fight it any longer. I just followed the lead that had been set and let my head ease its way onto my desk. I looked out the fourth-floor window at the gray cover of midmorning, watching the pigeons squawk about on the ledge and letting myself drift away.

I saw Will and Kevin standing at the end of the hall between fifth and lunch. It was the first time I'd seen either of them since the walk over to school in the morning. That walk had been awfully quiet. The three of us had been talked out from the night before. With the prospect of school hanging over us, we had nothing to say. Even when we stopped at the convenience store for coffee, we didn't speak. It was an understood silence.

But when I saw them there at the end of the hall

standing with Ryan and Taylor, I felt the need to talk to them. We'd spent over twelve hours the day before as a collective unit. When you go through all the phases of a trip with someone, you all kinda become one person . . you can't function without the other components. All day I'd had separation anxiety, like a twin who was missing his other halves.

I sauntered over like I knew I was the shit. The look on my face let others know that these were my boys loitering. Best to get out of my way because that's where I was heading.

My presence made the group complete. Will, me, Kevin, Taylor, and Ryan. That was our crowd. That's how everyone else saw us. And I guess that's sort of how we saw ourselves . . in terms of the whole and less as individuals.

"Oh shit, Brendon, where'd you come from? What's going on, Brendon?" Ryan said, being the first to see me move in, making the square they stood in more of a circle. I always liked that habit of his, the way he repeated your name with every new thing he had to say.

"Nothing!" I replied, more to everyone than to anyone special. Will and Kevin had just been relaying the sequence of events that summed up our night. Only they hadn't listed anything sequentially because acid doesn't allow the brain to remember the experience in a linear frame. Will had a number of clarifications for me to make, and they were all glad I had walked by. I filled in as many of the blanks as I could, bringing the story together for Ryan and Taylor.

The more we went on talking about it, the more we were laughing. Me and Kevin acting out our own parts while Will narrated. Ryan was saying how he wished he'd been there. And Taylor wondering why they hadn't been. I saw it in the slight frown that formed on his face. It was the look he always had when he thought he'd been left out. Truth was, we hadn't meant to exclude them. We hadn't thought about it. They simply weren't around in the split second we'd made our decision. Nothing intentional. Ryan could have given two shits. He thought it would have been fun, but it wasn't like he held anything against us. I could tell that Taylor kinda did.

Taylor looked over at Ryan. "Where were we yesterday?"

"I dunno, we went over to Mary's house and screwed around." By his tone, I knew Ryan saw what Taylor was getting at and was trying to cut him off. Taylor probably saw it, too, because he let it lie. And when it really comes down to it, it was Taylor's own fault. He'd wanted to go over to Mary's instead of hanging with us. She was his girlfriend and Will, Kevin, and I hated her guts. No way were we going, so we ended up just the three of us, and the rest is history.

"Ahh, we still should've gone," Taylor mumbled.

"It was a fucking riot, of course you should've gone." Good ol' Kevin, he always missed what was going on under the surface. His romance with narcotics always came shining through. But something about his attitude was infectious, and just as he'd gotten me over the hump the night before, he'd succeeded in breaking the tension. For the moment, Taylor was over the "where and why wasn't I there" and was back on the allure of pure sunshine. Our conversation lapsed back into a five-star acid review.

I was distracted though . . staring down the hall at all the strange faces and the ones that weren't so strange. My eye caught Plain Jane before anyone else had seen her. She rounded the corner heading right toward us . . Plain Jane with the face so lame. I didn't even know what the hell her real name was. Will and I always called her Jane. Even to her face, not that she ever knew why.

She spotted us, but it was already too late. I'd nudged Will right off. Jane was one of Sally's little friends. Now Sally's friends ain't as bold as her and not even close to being half as cute, so we didn't ever pay them any mind. Which meant they didn't really know us none. When we did bother to acknowledge their boring lives, it was purely to torment. Poor Jane never stood a chance.

She was walking by . . definitely Sally had told her a thing or two. That accounted for the look on young Jane's homely face once she noticed she'd walked smack into us. I saw her tense up. She always got frightened of us despite our pal Sally's pleas that we were harmless. But this time, Jane appeared more jittered than was usual.

Will must have noticed this, too, for when Jane got close he took the open opportunity. He jumped out from behind Ryan, who was tall and had hidden him rather well. He startled that girl straight crazy. I swear her skin near fell off her pointed bones.

He held her around the waist as we laughed. We all chanted "JANE! JANE! JANE!" Yelling right in her face.

"Get *off* me, you pervert," she whined, but those types of comments don't work past the sixth grade. We kept up the ritual incantation. "*Shut up*, that's not even my *name*!" she rebutted.

"It's your name now," I flat-out commanded.

It honestly was a mean game, the kind a bully would

play on the playground. But we were just trying to get some kicks and taunting people was about the only way to get them. Still, I guess it wasn't all that mean. Shit, Jane got to tell all her impressionable friends that she knew *us*.

People began hurrying past in a rush. Will released his prisoner. Saved by the bell had never been so true. She sort of sissy-hit him as she shook away. We laughed more and waved. I stood there thinking what kind of ass had decided that it would be a good idea for seventeen-year-olds to share time with fourteeners. Poor Jane. I took comfort in the belief that in three or four years she'd remember us and finally get it. She had spirit, so I was confident she would.

Ryan and Will and Taylor took off, leaving me and Kevin going the opposite way. But Kevin's class was a few doors down, so really I was alone again. I was headed to lunch, so I didn't have to worry about being late and all. I dragged my worn-out feet. God how I wanted to just curl up on a mat somewhere and take a nap. I debated walking right through the front doors and then right on home . . climbing into my unmade bed and then — just nothing. Hours of closed thoughts and nothing around. But the day was halfway over. I'd made it so far so good and lunch wasn't any big trick. I picked up my feet like a tired soldier and marched on over to the sickening smell of the lunchroom.

It hadn't taken much deliberation. Right before Jane livened things up a bit, we'd all agreed to take hits again that night. All of us this time. There was this party at a club over by the bus station. It was eighteen and older, but Ryan knew the bouncer and said he could get us in.

I was trying to figure out how the hell I was going to get any sleep between school and then. There was no way it was going to happen. Didn't matter, though, the acid would wake me up when the time came.

None of my real friends were in the cafeteria. Usually I sat with this group of stoners I didn't especially care for. Not feeling quite up to their company, I searched around for someone, anyone else. I was almost happy when I spied Sally on the far side of the room.

I was feeling pretty bad about the way we sometimes treated her. I decided to go sit at her table just to let her know Will and I weren't using her. I really did think she was alright, even if she was immature at times.

Her face lit up like a firefly when she saw me pull the chair out next to hers. She smiled real big, capturing the admiration of her friends. I could see it on their faces that my just being there was some sort of minor thrill. I enjoyed watching Sally wallow in the fame of it. She was the star of the day.

The others stared at me like I was some kind of celebrity. They were partially terrified, though. Each had that stung-by-the-headlights glare in their eyes, nervous as hell. I knew they spent countless hours trying to convince Sally that me and my friends were bad news.

I took up most of the lunch period thinking up things and making Sally laugh her ass off. All her bullshit friends didn't get it. Inside, I knew Sally wouldn't end up with those losers for long. She'd follow in our footsteps pretty soon. She'd carry on our legacy in this uptight school, because we were teaching her too much for her to just waste it.

I was being real careful not to lead Sally on. Last thing I wanted was for her to get some misinterpreted girlish dementia about a crush I would never have. I asked about her plans for the upcoming weekend. "Got any hot dates?" I asked.

I was surprised to hear Will was going to hang with her on Sunday. He'd never mentioned it, even though Sally claimed they'd had plans for days. That explained why he wanted to go over there the night before. Probably he didn't want to tell me, afraid it would've made me jealous. It didn't, so it was no big thing. I did, however, make a mental note to discuss this Sally situation with him later and make sure he didn't end up breaking her heart.

Out of the blue one of those mousy girls piped up. I could tell this girl had taken the whole lunch period to gather her courage to address me. "Why don't you call Marie by her name?" Her voice was so nasal and so snooty it made me physically ill.

"Who the hell is Marie?" I asked, completely irritated. I had no idea what she was talking about, and frankly I didn't care.

"*You* know," she was saying, "you guys all call her Jane."

So that was her real name. Go figure! I was in no mood to explain the sophistication of jokes or to carry on any further conversation with this brace-face, freckled girl. "HER NAME IS JANE!" was all I said. She didn't venture anything further after that.

I turned to Sally and asked her why she hung out with such troglodytes. I don't think Sally took too kindly to me insulting her friends. She gave me that "just leave them alone" look of hers, the one when the corner of her mouth sort of turns up.

I had wanted to ask her about real stuff, like her family or what she imagined herself being ten, twenty years from now. A hairdresser? A mother? A doctor? What? I had an urge to get to know her, but for some reason I couldn't form the questions. I had nothing but nonsense to offer. Whenever I got too close to getting personal with anyone my throat just kind of froze.

I'm not so sure why I had taken such a big brother attitude toward her all the sudden. It was probably due to my sleep deprivation. I *really* did think she was a swell girl. I was angry with myself for the contempt I had felt for her while standing outside her house. I hated acid-formed opinions. They leave bad impressions stuck in your head. I was working hard to change the one I'd formed of Sally.

THE FIRST TIME I EVER MET Will was in the little boys'
room. We were about eleven or less, but who can
remember such things. Will, for one, looked a hell of a
lot more on the side of less.

Wearing his overalls and his hair combed over in the
height of sixth-grade fashion, Will had a smile on his face
from the moment I opened the door . . probably even
before. I was going to walk past and take care of business
until he left, but he made the first move.

"Hey, check this out!" he said. I stopped, a bit surprised. Sure, we knew each other's faces and all, but we
didn't *know* each other and in middle school that means
you don't talk. Those were the rules. My mistake was
thinking that Will played by the rules. Will didn't *know*

the rules, let alone play by them. At eleven, it surprised me. Now it's one of the things about him that I respect and emulate.

Just us and a brand-new bathroom. The sink was one of those basin types. Horse trough kind. Will was standing over it and looking like trouble despite his size. Nothing can last at the disposal of hundreds of hormonal young boys. Damage is to be expected, and if it isn't, they're dumber than I give credit.

"I'm pluggin' up the drains!" Will squeaked out, and I heard his famous laugh for the first time. "Help me, why don't ya?"

Why not! It wasn't my usual style, but fuck it. We gathered scores of those rough brown paper towels and plastered them to the drain holes. The faucets were those push-and-drizzle-then-fade-away kind. So we had to keep rushing back and forth to keep them all going.

The basin was about a foot deep so it took some time, but we eventually won, you can bank on that! It was a slow fill, but as we ran out the door, the spillage ran onto the floor, leaving the flood in our wake for some tired janitor to mop up. It was the highlight of my day.

God, things were so easy in those days! Fun just found you out wherever you were. It wasn't all drugs this and drugs that. Now everything else seems so boring . . so not worth doing.

Plugging up drains and spoiling the bathrooms couldn't do it for us anymore. It's all politics after a while. Not maturity. No, it's fucking politics. It ain't hip to be into the minor destruction these days. These days it would be writing graffiti on the walls and tossing cigarette butts into the paint. That's the level we were on.

The fucking levels! Man, I hated all that shit. You pass through the stages of cool. That's how it is. We done passed through most! Doesn't leave much left for one to do. The worst part is that the levels have a way of getting at you. Will and I and all the rest of us had fallen victim. Following the path for spite, but following nonetheless.

We'd done the early pranks. The backtalk and the smart-ass cracks. We'd done the petty theft. Shoplifting for the cheap thrills. We had the property-damage covered. The harassment. The public nuisance. It's all the same. You take the next step once you've swum in the lower ranks. We'd grown too cool for this one or that one or whatever. You reach the top and then you do it all over again. High this time around and it's all new fun. But when you reach the top again? Then what? You reach the top on every kind of high and where's there to go?

That was our destination. A goal of sorts. Make the progression on up the line. But we were reaching the end in a flurry of psychedelic episodes. Breaking barriers and such. Hitting the panic stages with smiles and thin lines of drool on our faces. We'd grown too cool! Too cool for everything. Too cool for the whole scene. Too cool to even give a damn. So much of all the bullshit that happens in this school and at this age, we couldn't participate in because we'd done it before and passed through it. It was b-o-r-i-n-g! Worn-out and tired. Yawn, yawn, because we're on to the next big thing.

That's how we knew we were better than all the rest of this world. At least, that's what we thought. But as I stood in the bathroom thinking back on it all, I wasn't so sure. It would be nice if something so stupid as flooding the sinks could hold some semblance of fun for me now. But it doesn't. It just depresses me.

It gets me down if I let it . . if I let my mind drift back to what was then and drift forward to what's ahead. Things drop off. It's hard to find interest in anything after a time. Christ, we couldn't even enjoy the harmless hangout. Everything had to be an adventure . . an assault on the senses. It makes it hard to communicate with people. I mean, they're all about the weather, the nice new sweater and all that small talk. I can't deal with trivialities. Every conversation needs to be substantial. Every word! Every fucking gesture! Or forget about it. What's the point? You're not on my level. You're not cool enough for me.

Man, it really gets me down. When everything's exhausted there's nothing left. The rate I was running, it wouldn't be long. Then what? What's next? What's the score? I can't handle the rest of my life suspended in boredom. Such a chore! Gonna burn out because I can't stand to fade away. Get it all in fast and get out. No turning back now. It's just the way it is, the way I need to be.

I dipped my hands under the cold, rusty water. Crumpled up the towel and tossed it. *Fuck it*, I thought as I pushed through the door and into a million fractions of conversation.

BY THE LAST CLASS OF THE DAY, I was getting my fifth wind. It was the period I looked forward to every day. Not because it was last either. I wasn't one of those "school sucks" socialite types who counted the minutes of the day. Well, maybe that day I was, but that was simply due to fatigue. Normally I never really minded school that much.

I looked forward to last period because it was English, which I really dug. And because Will was in it along with Melissa. It was one of the advanced classes, the nerd class, but by some stroke of luck Will and I managed to get into the same one.

Our teacher was this real intelligent guy. One of those Vietnam protest types. From the first day he'd taken a friendly liking to Will and me. I guess he saw in us a certain affinity with his own glory days. Occasionally we stayed after class to talk further with him, discussing books that would never find their way into the high school curriculum. I remember the first day when he told us to call him Wally instead of Mr. Rhodes. Man, that blew us away. It was about the coolest fucking thing a teacher had ever said to me. It had taken a few days until Will and I were comfortable with it, but once we were, that's exactly what we called him. Not in class, though, just during the forty minutes or so we'd spend with him after school.

When I walked into the room, there was hardly anybody there yet. I did a quick survey to make sure I hadn't missed Melissa or Will. I hadn't. Neither of them were there, so I took a seat by the door so I could catch whichever of them happened to enter first.

Secretly I had hoped Melissa would get there before Will. I still desperately desired a few moments alone with her. Finding out that Will had already made plans with Sally for the weekend had stirred the competitiveness within me. It was like I had to prove to him that I could get a girl, too, that I wasn't jealous like he thought I was. If Melissa had only showed up first, I might've been able to salvage the weekend. But she didn't. I saw Will turning into the doorway, wearing a smile and my shirt.

"Hey!" he said, truly excited to see me. And for an instant I felt guilty for wishing he hadn't shown up.

I could tell Will was in a giddy mood, acting like he'd just gotten away with smoking a cigarette in the lavatory or something. I quickly found my own happiness growing in measured increments.

"What's up?" I asked.

"Nothing, except . . *we're gonna do some acid later!*" We both laughed, and I jokingly told him I'd forgotten all about that.

Will was telling me how I could go back to his house after school and catch some sleep. His mom would still be at work so we wouldn't be bothered. I halfheartedly agreed because right then I spotted Melissa coming in.

She had on this top that fit perfectly around that goddesslike figure of hers, capturing the beauty of every curve. It was tucked carefully into a pleated skirt that hung freely around her knees. God, I was a sucker for skirts. There was just something so feminine and so downright sexy about 'em. And her eyes . . so full of caring and so green like the lawns in some imagined heaven. Her whole person took my breath away. I motioned to say hello, but stopped short when I noticed she hadn't even looked in my direction.

That was it. Another week gone by and another week

in which I'd failed to ask Melissa out. I tried telling myself it wasn't my fault. I had such a small window of time, only the five or so minutes before class on Friday. I couldn't very well ask her out before then. If she said no before last period on a Friday, so what? I could deal with a half hour of embarrassment because by Monday it would all be like pollution washed under the bridge.

Will being there didn't help things much. He knew I had a thing for Melissa and always tried to talk me out of it. He thought she was okay, but definitely not all that. Due to his less-than-ardent approval, I never committed to telling him how I was absolutely wild about her. Only Kevin knew because he was more open to those kinds of things. He didn't judge girls like Will did.

Around him I had to keep up my image more, which meant taking a casual manner toward Melissa during English class. But man, I wish I could've talked to her then. It was a perfect lead-in to something more substantial than a hello. It was a subject I could discuss with her and feel fairly confident that I wasn't making a complete ass of myself. But sometimes you just gotta sacrifice for the sake of friends.

I was feeling a little awful. The acid was most likely responsible. It uses up all the good stuff during the trip and leaves all the poison behind to hit you the next day. Not a flashback, though — that I could deal with. Flashbacks were like getting a little extra for your money. That definitely wasn't what I was feeling. It was more like the mind getting itself reacquainted with a linear form of thinking.

Good ol' Wally was preaching the power of imagination, singing its praises to us creative students. But I wasn't feeling the same way about it. My imagination was taking me on a bad ride. I was imagining myself as a wilted old man eating dry cereal in a rundown, rented room. I could see the rocking chair as my ancient body tried hard to sway it. I could even smell the puddle of piss in the corner where the mice lived. That "wonderful imagination" of mine was doing nothing except succeeding to get me into an asylum for the clinically depressed.

We had been studying *The Rime of the Ancient Mariner* for the last few days. When I read it, it touched me somewhere deep. I felt like that mariner sometimes, no connections to anything. But then, everybody in the world probably felt that way at some point or another. I was no one special.

"*Alone, alone, all, all alone,/ Alone on a wide wide sea!*" That's what Coleridge wrote nearly two hundred years ago. And looking over at the separation between desks . . between my desk and Will's and mine and Melissa's, I was struck by just how valid those words really were.

Later, I might tell Will these thoughts, if only to get the comfort of that nod of his. Just thinking about it was a relief. At that moment I really believed that his subtle gestures were about the only things keeping me from drowning in that "*wide wide sea.*"

I turned around to look at him. He raised his eyebrows, wondering what I was thinking. I just smiled, and he grinned back. That was all. That's all I needed. I went back to listening to Wally's lecture. I have no idea what Will thought I was thinking, but it didn't matter. I was feeling insecure and needed his reassurance, and he'd given it without even knowing.

We didn't stay after to chat with Wally. We *did* go out of our way to say good-bye and have a nice weekend, however. I also made the effort to stop Melissa on her way out. I asked how she'd been. She said something along the lines of "Fine, and you?" but what she said wasn't what was really important; getting her to talk was what mattered.

It was a strained conversation on my end. I hoped she hadn't noticed that I was wearing what Will wore the day before and vice versa. I had thought about asking her to join us tonight but . . Christ, how ridiculous would it sound? "Wanna get mad fucked up with me tonight? Go to this club and do drugs?" I'd come off sounding like a stoner from some bad movie made in the 70s.

Melissa was too sophisticated for our underworld tastes. She would never get into that scene. "Why do you go to those places?" she asked me once. I still don't know how to answer. It's a search for the surreal . . for the next wave. She was more into the real. Hadn't yet made it to the point where the real holds no value. She'd ask why we don't just hang out. I've already been through all that.

Too hard to explain, so we just stood and bullshitted for a few seconds until her friends arrived and shuffled her off. God, I was such a coward! Why was it I could flirt with every dip-shit girl I couldn't care less about and then not be able to bring myself to say even one interesting thing to the girl I was in love with? I stumbled and babbled because I couldn't bring myself to small talk, but I had nothing else to say. Once we had been close enough to cry in front of each other, and now . . it was like I had to script every word I said.

It wasn't for a few minutes, until Kevin came by, that I was able to get over my self-pity.

"You coming over?" Will asked Kevin as he got near enough to hear.

"Naw, I should go home."

"Alright. Then we'll see you later? We'll go over to your place after we get up."

Kevin was fine with that, so the plan was set. Go to Will's and get some much-needed sleep, then over to Kevin's and from there meet up with Taylor and Ryan. It sounded sane enough, so Kevin took his leave.

Will and I walked slowly down the hall and out into the street. The sun had come out by then, but it wasn't like summertime, when blue skies were warming. It was that late autumn kind of sun that never made any sense because there was still a chill in the breeze. I always found the sunshine to be depressing when it was cold. It just didn't match the weather.

I searched the skyline for something to say. My focus went from near to far, north to south. I found nothing of interest. It was still the same town I'd always known. Philly — Drug City, PA. The perfect combination of modern and archaic.

"Got anything to eat at your house? I don't have any money to waste and I'm starving!"

Will looked at me, debating my question. I could tell he was going through a mental inventory of his refrigerator and pantry, wracking his brain to come up with something appetizing. He shrugged his shoulders, saying, "We got bacon and mayo. We could make toast."

"Sounds good to me. Let's go then. Pick your sorry feet up and move, bitch!" I teased. Will took off, practically running. I had to make an extreme effort just to catch up with him. It killed me how he could go at a slow suburban pace and then break like a flash without notice. I think I laughed the whole way back to his house.

I was completely out of breath when Will turned the key and swung open his front door. We had run the entire route, not that it was far or anything, but we had run it at top speed. I immediately smelled the musty scent that came through the door.

Will and his mom lived in a duplex apartment with a streetside entrance. There were many rooms that remained unfurnished and unused on account it was only the two of them and it was huge. I always had the feeling I was in a dead person's house, and no matter how hard I tried to shake it, I couldn't.

Will and I went straight into the kitchen without even taking off our coats. We made the bacon sandwiches we had been craving and ate them greedily. Satisfied for the moment, we commenced with the formality of taking off our jackets and throwing them on the floor in one of the empty living rooms.

I was just about to follow Will up the stairs into his room when I remembered to call my mom and let her I know I was alive and well.

My mom was in a pleasant enough mood on the phone. Still, I heard the faint air of suspicion creep in once I told her I probably wouldn't be coming home that night. When she had asked why not, I made up some lie that I couldn't remember two minutes later. I hoped she thought we were all going to go get drunk or something. Hell, if she confronted me in the morning, that's even what I'd tell her we did. Alcohol's one thing — LSD, that's a whole other story. I was so out of it that I almost forgot to tell her I loved her.

I hung up the phone and my brain fixed itself on the image of uninterrupted slumber. I walked into Will's room, where he was already lying down. He had his Firehouse Jazz compilation album on. Tom & Jerry Jazz we called it because it sounded like cartoon theme music. It sounded just like liquid to the ears and I drank in every note.

"*Man!*" I said. "What a lullaby."

Will opened one of his closed eyes and smiled his famous smile. He positioned himself over to the far left side of his queen-size bed and motioned for me to take the right side. I relished the prospect of snoozing on a yielding bed instead of the solid, unforgiving floorboards.

Kevin never would've gotten into that bed. "What am I, gay?" I heard him saying. He was so uncomfortable with things like that. So what if people thought that? The whole point was to not give a shit what people thought. Will and I couldn't care less. We were both tired. We both wanted to sleep on a bed and there was plenty of room. And so what if his arm wandered in its sleep and happened to touch me? It was only touch, and touch ain't nothing.

I let the music dance its merry way into the cerebrum. It was going to be a busy night, so I had to make the most of the time allotted. I explored the passages of my brain until I found that secluded dream chamber and lingered there. I let my body fall into the pattern of Will's snoring. And then nothing. Nothing all around me, like a favorite blanket.

I DREAMED OF BLUE CHILDREN AND wild gardens. Flowers made of moonbeams and old-man speech mixed into the wind like records of high-quality production. Silver water and purple clouds that I could eat and feed on.

That's the world I was always looking for. I just had to keep believing it, keep dreaming it, and someday I'd find myself there for real. I'd travel by faith alone. I'd travel through insanity. I'd live the beggar's life. And it would all be worth it because the reward was golden fields and an army of rats parading behind the music my flute made as I piped along.

It's the kind of dream that's found in the spirals of smoke and beneath the cracks in the sidewalk. It leaves you floating like a god, above the world on the back of some giant turtle with the gift of flight.

One day I'll wake in a shanty slum beneath an overpass. The sound of the highway ringing in my ears. The doll with white claws cuddled in my arms. Then I'll know that I'm there, because that's the way this dream begins.

But that's not where I woke. And the claws were Amos the cat's and not from the worn doll.

The room was dark. The cat was driving me crazy with the scratching and the pawing and I wanted to up-and-kick it hard. Will was in the shower from what I could gather from the light showing through under the door and the sound of rushing water not unlike the sounds that cars make in the distance, above one's scope of hearing.

So it was this now. The waiting. Phone calls back and forth and tracking people down like FBI. I hated this part. I wanted the night to begin. I needed none of this anticipation. None of the arranging of plans and such. Just get it together and skip all this shit for Christ's sake! The longer the wait, the farther away the dream went.

I sat passive in front of Will's fish tank. Watching the buggers swim here and there and then dip to hide in the comfort of a tiny cave. I had taken a fancy to this baby-bluish fish. There was something subdued about her, about the way she swam and about the way she ignored the rest of them. She reminded me of Melissa, in about as much as a fish can remind someone of a person, I guess.

Back and forth and here and there and all the rest. I watched until I got depressed. I was feeling the itch. I couldn't sit still much longer, it was driving me nuts. Still and quiet. Still and quiet. It's a recipe for bringing you down. God I just wanted to get going!

And then Will came out of the bathroom. I looked at him, he smiled, but we didn't have much to say. I tilted my head and he nodded so it was understood. I took my leave and took my turn in the steam of a nice, hot shower and a chance at getting clean.

ADAM'S ONE-ROOM APARTMENT RESEMBLED something out of a television program. He had six chains on the door and a stolen fire hydrant resting in the corner. The whole place was filled with the presence of Ryan, Will, Kevin, Taylor, and me. He didn't usually let his customers drop by without any notice, but we went way back. He had gone to school with us before he graduated two years before. Therefore we could come knocking whenever the need struck.

After all the locks were secured, he asked us what we wanted. We told him we each wanted hits and that he might as well throw in an eighth of weed while he was at it. It always amazed me the way his house was an all-night supermarket for drugs.

Holding a dropper full of rust-colored liquid up to the light, Adam looked at us. "You gentlemen sure you don't want any of this instead?"

"Whatcha got in there, Adam?" Ryan asked, squinting up his eyes to get a clearer picture.

"Liquid LSD, my friends. Just press your finger to the outside of this container and you'll be tripping for two days!"

That sounded like a nightmare to me. I hated Adam right then for making a push. It was out of character for him and it wasn't working either. The only reason we dealt with him in the first place was because he didn't do shit like that. I guess he thought this was a special product worthy of a sales pitch. Drug dealers annoyed the hell out me sometimes.

"Ahhh, no thanks. We'll just take the regular strength," Ryan said, and we all voiced our agreement.

"Works for me," and Adam carefully placed the bottle back on the table. He handed each of us a little sewing baggy made to hold a single button. In them were those longed-for squares of paper with Day-Glo suns illustrated on them. In the spirit of exchange and commerce, we all handed over wrinkled Abe Lincolns, all except Kevin who had five Washingtons instead.

Adam stood staring at us like he was waiting for us to

leave. Kevin and I looked over at each other with an expression that communicated a likeness of thought. Finally, Taylor spoke up, "The weed? An eighth, remember?"

Adam exaggerated the shock on his face in order to make it seem funny to us that he certainly had forgotten. We laughed out of courtesy, but really we were getting a little pissed off. I was, anyway. Adam was just rubbing me the wrong way the whole time. I wanted to get our shit and get out. No "let's be pals." No chitchat.

Adam had gone into his drawer where his stash was kept. His hand reached in, returning with a nice-size bag of good grass. He handed it over to Taylor who somehow always ended up with the weed. Adam told us it was on the house. He could be such a businessman sometimes.

On the way out he asked us if we had any interest in counterfeit twenties. "Only if I can pay you with them!" Kevin called out over his shoulder as we left. Adam laughed uneasily as he locked the door behind us.

When we'd gotten halfway down the block and out of earshot, I turned to face everyone. "Jesus Christ, what the hell was up with him?"

"What do you mean?"

I could tell by his face that Ryan really hadn't noticed anything. "He was acting like a fucking asshole, that's what I mean. Playing the big-shot drug dealer, trying to show off."

"Oh, *was* he?" Ryan asked the rest, not wanting to fully trust me without checking out the other opinions.

Taylor was the first to speak. He looked more at me than at Ryan when he said, "He was *probably* fucked up. I don't think he meant anything by it."

"No excuse!" I meant it, Adam had really pissed me off.

"He's just an asshole, that's all. No reason for it." And with that, Kevin had put an end to it. I sure as hell couldn't argue with him. He had this way of stating his opinions like they were proven facts, and most of the time I thought they might as well have been.

We walked a few blocks without speaking. I felt the mood lapsing for no reason. It's like that when there's a group and no one's speaking. It gets uncomfortable. I was beginning to worry about the rest of the night . . and worry isn't a good prelude to tripping. It sort of gets the whole mind flowing in the wrong direction. I needed a switch in groove before it got too late for changing.

We could all feel it, but nobody did anything about it. Finally, Will raised his glance from the ground. He stopped walking and stood until we all stopped and looked at him.

He spoke softly, certain of the reception he would receive from the suggestion he was about to put forth. "Hey guys, let's head over to the park and smoke some of that free weed. Huh? What do you say?"

Conversation rushed right back into us as the cigar paper burned down. It had been Ryan's idea to stop at the store and pick up a blunt. Philly brand, naturally. We all needed cigarettes anyway, so it only made sense. Taylor was eighteen, which made the purchase easy.

It had been my idea to take the tabs while in the store. I told everyone that I thought the fluorescent lights would make the experience all the more memorable for posterity. In addition, the utter illegality of it was exhilarating. Taylor had paid the cashier as the paper dissolved in his mouth. On the way out, Will even stuck out his tongue at the man, exhibiting our crime for his amusement.

The park was an atmosphere of comfort. There were people all around but we didn't care. We had grown arrogant. Some of them would look over, and when they did, it made me nervous. But we had done the same routine so many times that if asked, we probably would have said it was legal. We were more afraid that people would want us to share with them than we were of them squealing to the police.

The five of us were sitting on benches arranged in a quad. I was appreciating the difference between marijuana smoked while waiting for the acid to kick in instead of on the wind-down. By doing it this way, the strychnine buildup is blurred. The weed eases the body into the trip like an on-ramp eases traffic onto the highway.

Every time a person would walk close by, we'd all break down. Each time we saw someone new approaching, we dared one another to keep quiet. It became a test of self-control. We failed miserably. We just couldn't keep it in no matter how hard we tried. All it took was one of us to bust and the rest would follow.

We were becoming a regular nuisance, lying across benches and shouting obscenities. It got to the point where middle-aged couples would steer their children in the opposite direction.

We tried convincing ourselves that we were invisible. "If you don't move, they can't see you!" Ryan was saying. But we couldn't stay still, so everyone went right on seeing us.

At one point I even got up and went over and sat down

right next to this old lady. The guys could all see what I was doing and they were shouting things across the way. I knew the old lady heard them, but she never let on. I was pulling my famous Hamlet act, putting on like I was crazy. I let a sliver of drool run a course down my chin and let the foam fill my mouth like I had rabies. I started slapping my knee real hard with the back of my hand. Then I let out a horrendous series of laughs at top volume. I was carrying on like a genuine lunatic.

Over my own roar I could hear the guys laughing something fierce. The old woman must have thought we were stark raving mad. I leaned a little more toward her, my screams echoing through her ears. She gave a slight shake of the head and I pictured her mumbling silently to herself something about the state of young people these days. She rose right up, shifting weight onto her brittle bones. She never even looked in my direction! She just got up and hobbled away. I slipped out of character and fell into convulsions.

Kevin took up the entertainment where I left off. He had seen the way the old lady was clutching her handbag and recognized it as a point of entry. "That's right! Run along, you old hag!" he was yelling. "Think I'm gonna snatch your purse? Huh? Whatever! I don't want your tired-ass junk!"

We were all dying. Later, if I thought about it again, I might feel bad about disturbing that poor woman's peace, but as it was happening I was too caught up in the comedy of it. That's the way it is when you lived like we did. The world is a playground for your recreation and everything and everyone in it are just props at your disposal.

I stood as soon as I got my senses back. Walking over to rejoin the group, I noticed the variations in my vision. The acid was creeping into my bloodstream like a plague. I completely forgot that smoking weed accelerates the machination of the heart valves, thus quickening the introduction of LSD to the brain. I couldn't tell where the effects of one drug were giving way to the other. I had the faint sensation that I was flying, or at least hovering a few inches above the ground.

I heard Will through a fog. He looked at me, saying, "Sit down before you fall down." He must have seen me wobble, or else I actually *was* floating above the ground. I didn't respond, too lost in my revolving thoughts of optical stimulation.

"SIT DOWN BEFORE YOU FALL DOWN!" all four of them were now repeating in a southern drawl. They sounded so distant. I couldn't bring myself to sit. My muscles tightened at the thought. I was too caught up in the movement of the stars overhead and the strength of the pigeon's wings that flew in front of them. I spread my arms like a scarecrow, watching for the clouds to move in.

It took some convincing but I did manage to get them all off their asses. It was going on ten-thirty and I was getting the fever to be inside somewhere. The prospect of the club rested on our minds like the promise of heaven did for devoted Christians. We headed there with a bounce in our step.

I lingered back a few feet behind the rest, staring at the litter that blew around in the streets. I found myself fascinated by a piece of newspaper caught in the backdraft of opposing winds. To my altered perception, it appeared to stand still in the air. It was unnerving. I wiggled my fingers at that paper like a witch casting a spell, believing I had some magical control over nature. It was actually more disturbing when it worked and the paper took off once again. I was too fucked up to grasp the concept of coincidence and way too freaked out to watch where the newspaper traveled from there.

I tried to avoid looking any of the others in the eye.

Everyone was now wearing his acid face, and I hadn't adjusted yet. I took to watching the sidewalk instead. With the insect sensitivity the LSD had bestowed on me, I noticed the slight imperfections in the cement. I saw the color shifts from one slab to the next. Like gasoline rainbows on the road in summertime, they disappeared once I was on top of them.

I quickened my step to catch up with Will. He looked over at me and smiled. I could tell he was struggling with an identical lack of reality.

He was fumbling with something in his hand. I asked him what it was. He smiled again, but this time absent-mindedly. He opened his hand to reveal a fragment of shattered glass. Its edges were dangerously sharp. Kevin saw it, too.

"Jesus, what the hell are you doing?" he asked.

Will just kinda laughed like he was trapped in a movie. "I dunno," he said, throwing the glass to the concrete and seeing it break into a million pieces. It was a beautiful display, and the three of us watched in appreciation as the particles scattered.

"I'm a mess!" I said to them.

Taylor must've of heard me because he spun around like he was made of clay, startling the hell out of us. "I'M TRIPPING MY FUCKING FACE OFF!" he exclaimed in absolute exhilaration. He continued to animate his features until I thought we were all going to piss our pants with laughter.

Ryan was the only one keeping his cool about him. Drugs never affected Ryan in the same way. It was like his parents had inoculated him against their influence when he was younger. The rest of us were losing our minds and there was Ryan, calm and collected.

I teased him a little about it, just to get him involved in the action. "Ryan, what's the matter?" I asked. "You're acid beat or something? What's going on?"

"Naw, I'm good."

Kevin and I shook our heads in total admiration. The man was made of iron. Tough as nails. I looked at him again and he flashed me an open-mouthed grin. The proportions of his face were so distorted by my sight that he momentarily resembled a giant monkey. I laughed out loud and Ryan laughed right along with me, not even knowing what was so funny.

It wasn't long before we were standing right outside the club. The music was penetrating through the walls so we could hear it clearly. The bass grabbed me in the chest and set the rate at which my heart beat. I held back a minute while Ryan straightened everything out with the bouncer.

I had underestimated the consequences of tripping two nights in a row. It felt like the new acid had resurrected the old from hibernation so that both could mingle in chemical intercourse.

I wasn't sure if I was prepared to enter the crowded club. Granted, everyone in there would be high in some form or another, but still the thought of all those intoxicated bodies made me claustrophobic.

Ryan turned toward us and motioned us along. "No turning back now," I whispered so no one but me could hear it.

Inside, the place was very dark . . only the occasional strobe or cluster of candles to light the place. The sound was intense. I felt the electronic beats pulsing through my veins like medicine. And as the security guy patted us down, I was struck with the idea that we were explorers boarding a vessel propelled by music. Once locked inside the capsule, we would be shuttled across time and space and would arrive in some future galaxy. This idea appealed to me. With dilated eyes, I strode boldly into the smoke-filled atmosphere.

THE CLUB HAD ONE MAIN DANCE floor with little cubical rooms and couches off to the side. Speakers as tall as me were arranged at every angle. The sound pulsing from them was tangible, filling the enclosed space with sonic waves. I felt my joints shift with each cut in the record the DJ created.

There were hundreds of people swarming all around. Every one of them was dressed in the height of fashion. Men and women alike, decked out in fur coats and eye makeup. Shoes with five-inch heels tapped the wood floor in rhythm. Eyes and skin tone of every ethnicity were woven into the chaos. The spectrum of color generated from the clothing was beautiful to behold . . and the smell of moist fabric was everywhere.

I was styling in my own way. I had on this orange polyester shirt I'd borrowed from Will. It fit real tight around my chest, exaggerating the thinness. Butterfly collar to the maximum, and cuffs that hung away from the wrists. I remembered picking it out and thinking the bright color would be perfect.

As I opened up my coat, Kevin looked over and started cracking up. "Damn," he said, "where'd you get them threads at? Looks like you stole that right out of an after-school special!"

"Close enough," I said. "I took it from Will's closet!"

"Brendon, you didn't tell us you were going all out. What? You trying to show us up or something?"

I looked at Ryan, who was dressed in the usual manner, a pair of khakis and a Gilligan striped sweater. I looked over at the rest and they were all in similar attire. It was the first any of them besides Will had seen me. I hadn't taken off my coat before then because I wanted to give them all a little surprise when they were tripping. They all sort of relied on me to be a little crazy. Since I never gave a shit what anyone but them thought, anyway, I was always happy to oblige.

Kevin, Ryan, and Taylor were smiling, still getting used to the sight of me when I spoke up again. "Now that's not all by any means. Check this out." I reached into my coat pocket, scrounging for the yellow-lens sunglasses inside. When I found them, I put them on. The image was complete. I cut the figure of an LSD poster boy to perfection. The tint of the shades matched up with the color of my hair and magnified the finery of the shirt.

I held my wide-eyed head high with a broad smirk extending from cheek to cheek. From one look at me, everyone in that sorry club knew I was the fucking disco king. Mr. Friday Night with an acid grin. I would be the admiration of all those suburban kids in from Jersey. If I came back the next week, I'd change my style up. I had to keep it fresh from appearance to appearance. I knew the next time I went there, there would be at least three fakers looking exactly like I did tonight.

Almost immediately after we got settled inside, we spotted a few scenesters we recognized. Taylor was always trying to bring outsiders into our group, so he led us over to them.

When I got close enough to see who it was we were meeting up with, I saw that I knew them, too. It turned out to be Phoebe, Vanessa, and Mikey . . three waster types I couldn't care less about. I looked over at Will, rolling my eyes. I could tell he wasn't in the mood to deal with them either. Begrudgingly, we took our seats on the sofa and observed the conversation.

I smoked a cigarette in a casual fashion, vaguely concentrating on the voices involved in a shouted dialogue. I let my gaze wander onto the dance floor. I let my mind fade into the pattern of the strobes . . blinking accordingly.

I caught a whiff of the Magic Marker smell as a cloud of PCP smoke went up beside me. I knew it was Mikey without even looking. It had to be. Every time I'd ever seen that kid he was dusted to the eyeballs. No one else I knew shared his habit, so he always ended up smoking it all by himself. He thought it was so goddamn exotic. His brain was hot-wired from inhaling all that shit. It was kind of sad the way he was on the long-and-winding road down. Christ, he couldn't even speak in full sentences anymore. He was likely to die of an aneurysm at any time. I never could understand why Taylor insisted we associate with addicts like that.

One thing I could be sure of, the acid was in full swing. I was feeling an amnesia of the senses. The night was lingering on the edge of decadence, and the world was colored yellow by the filtering lenses in front of my eyes. The cigarette in my hand had burned its way down to the filter. I let it fall onto the floor, enchanted by the slow motion flight of the ashes as they fell.

* * *

Will, Taylor, and myself were having our familiar bunny-kitten debate. We all had this theory that all females fit into one of four categories in the same way food fit into the four food groups. There were the girls whose faces resembled bunny rabbits with cute noses and round eyes. Then there was the type that looked more like cats . . small triangular faces and large eyes. The ones with long noses and flat features fit into the horse category, and all the short, ugly girls were remaindered into the troll department. Every once in a while there'd be a girl whose beauty would shoot the whole theory to hell because it was indescribable. Those girls we fit into the alien slot because they were just too good to be human.

I subscribed to the bunny club. Though felines were attractive, too, it was the bunny girls who blew me away. So damn cute, every last one of them. My philosophy had been that I would take a kitten if she came my way, but if given the choice, I'd take the rabbit type without a second thought.

Will had a preference for the felines. He was religious about it. I had never seen him with a girl that didn't fall unquestionably into the kitten section. No one I knew cared too much for the horses or the trolls, but I knew there were some guys out there who did, because I'd seen countless numbers of those types walking arm in arm with some poor loser.

We were having a good time classifying the girls at the club as they passed by. I pointed at one girl standing nearby. "She's a troll."

"Trolls are nasty!" Taylor added in between spurts of laughter. I wanted to tell him that I thought his girlfriend, Mary, was a troll but I didn't think it would go over too well.

I looked over my shoulder to check on Kevin and Ryan. They'd been talking up Phoebe and Vanessa ever since Mikey had passed out. They saw me looking and waved me over. I took my leave of Will and Taylor and stumbled to where they were sitting.

"We were thinking about getting a second hit," Ryan said.

"Really!" I was stunned. I'd barely been able to control the effect of the first one and I wasn't even at full peak. I gave Kevin a slight twist of face to silently question him. He answered back with a wink of the eye, communicating that he had every intent of going through with the plan.

It didn't really surprise me that Ryan would buy another. He was an acidhog due to the drug's limited influence on him. He had a higher tolerance than I did. Hell, I'd been with him before when he was on three hits and he was just as at ease as if he'd been sober. But Kevin? I was flat-out stunned. I mean, honestly, we had just tripped the night before, how much did he think he could handle?

"You're really gonna drop another?" I asked again.

"Yeah, I think so," Ryan said. "What do you think, Brendon, you wanna get one, too?"

Truth was, it did sound tempting. But after I had the chance to digest the utter insanity of the proposal, I told them no. My mind already felt like it was expanding at a rate I couldn't control. No need to rush it along on a crash course.

The way it turned out, Taylor joined them on a two-hit odyssey. Will was with me all the way. He told me he could already taste the bile in his stomach and didn't want to end up leaving a trail of intestines from the club all the way back to his house.

The three of them got up to walk around in search of a dealer with ready supply. I knew it shouldn't be too hard to find. The whole club stunk with the traffic of illicit substances. Everywhere you'd turn, some drug violation or another was taking place. There were speed freaks sniffing lines right out of the palms of their hands . . college girls caught in the shameless grip of Ecstasy . . suppressed violent types under the false strength of PCP. In a way it was sickening. I dreaded the thought of ever becoming the kind of person that lived from one high to the next. Sometimes I believed I might end up that way on the drugs because once you're doing them, then you're really fucking doing them! Everything else pales in comparison. Nothing comes near the narcotic fun, the paradise of sensation and such. But I was sure that death would claim me and wash all my sins away before it ever got to that point. I'd make certain of it if I had to.

Before the others returned, I got up on the pretense of getting a drink of water. I was feeling the need to walk around and test out my legs. As I made my way to the bar, I spied this real pretty Asian girl. Her face had the perfect coloring and texture of doll plastic. She was wearing a bright yellow tank top that looked like it was made of rubber. She had matched it with a plaid skirt that really covered no more than what a modest pair of underwear might. And she stood there just like a goddess without shame, practically naked in front of everyone.

One look at her and I could tell she was one of the Neo-Tokyo types. She was one of those girls who envied the allure of Hello Kitty products and the seduction of the unreal. She had a felt ribbon in her shining black hair and her whole person looked like it was taken right from some Japanimation movie.

I decided that I had nothing to lose by just going to talk to her. The ungoverned atmosphere of the club emboldened me. I told myself that I was looking good, what with my fancy getup and the shades and such. The flow of hallucinogens to the brain had left me devoid of any self-doubt.

"Where you from?" I asked by way of introduction. I was practically standing on top of her. She must have thought I was a real fucking basket case with the pupils of my eyes bugging out of their sockets like they were.

She gave me the look of a snob. Before I had opened my stupid mouth, she had been giving me the encouraging eye. Or at least I thought she had. She probably thought I was cute before I approached her and made a complete ass out of myself.

I couldn't believe it when I heard myself asking if she came there often. What was I, some second-rate

Hollywood actor? I immediately wanted to take it back, but it was too late. The damage was already done. I desperately wanted to say something else. Anything else! But I just stood there staring at her like a little boy with puppy eyes. I wanted her to reach out and touch my hand, to do anything that would wipe the dumb look from my face. But all she did was turn her nose up at me and walk away. I couldn't really blame her, though. I came off like a pervert or a creep at best and it most certainly weirded her out.

I made a mental note to myself to avoid any attempts to pick up girls for the rest of the night. My condition had obviously deteriorated to a level where that type of activity would be doomed to failure.

I found myself seated in an obscure corner on the edge of the polished wood dance floor. I had made my way across the busy room, pushing and being pushed from behind. My mood had taken a drastic dive. The flood tide had reached the banks of my mind and I felt the waning presence of reality.

There was this guy, tall and thin, and he was dancing in place a few feet in front of me. His knotted hair was pulled back and tied behind his neck. The thick cluster of dreads sat like a headdress atop his head, diminishing the apparent size of his face. His long-limbed body kept in a constant repetitive motion, like someone performing a tribal ritual.

From the contour of his bare shoulders to the tips of his elongated fingers, the guy's body approximated the shape of a lizard. His dance remained in an instant replay sequence. I saw sweat run down the bridge of his nose only to fly off during a rapid change in direction. He had a case of the windup sickness . . stuck in the rhythm of the music's quickness.

The flash of the strobe lights was creating a dizzying sensation as my eyes skipped from second to second. I sat like one enchanted by a snake charmer's flute or an old sailor's seafaring tale. I was too terrified to move, afraid that I would cease to exist if the spell were broken. So I stayed put, isolated in an obscure corner of a crowded place.

Slowly, I let my mind relax and felt my dreams develop matter . . felt the melting away of feeling and the embrace of the water within me.

* * *

Will was practically sitting in my lap. I hadn't even registered his coming over toward me. Having lost all track of linear time, I had no idea how long I had been staring at the fluid motions of the liquid dancers. And I had only a vague recollection of the imaginary world I had so recently inhabited.

The touch of Will's warm hand hit me like an electric circuit at high voltage. My whole field of vision was shattered. It was a relief when my eyes finally settled their focus on Will's grinning features.

He asked if I was okay and I told him that I couldn't be absolutely sure because I wasn't currently sure who I was to begin with. We both got a good laugh out of that.

Back down on planet Earth, I was made abruptly aware that I was tripping hard. Harder than I had in a long time, due to the previous night's excursion and the small dose of slumber in between.

Will's nearness had begun to freak me out a little bit. His face was so close to mine that it wouldn't have taken any effort for him to extend his narrow tongue and lick my cheek. During the height of a trip I needed the comfort of distance. Didn't want anyone near enough to touch. But I also feared Will would mistake my intentions if I asked him to move and I most definitely didn't want a hurting of feelings.

I took several deep breaths and with each I grew more accustomed to Will's proximity. He looked me straight in the eye with a beaming smile to express his far gone mental state. And I felt the old playground feeling like I was rocking on a swing with a friend doing the same beside me. I started to enjoy my trip again.

"Where are the other guys?" I asked.

"What do you mean where?" Returning my question with a more complicated one. Normally, I would have been annoyed by such a response but under the circumstances I had begun to chuckle.

"I mean, *where* are the other guys? Kevin? Taylor? Ryan? *Where* are they or are they nowhere and I just made them up in my head?"

Will's face went blank for a second. "What?" he said, starting to laugh and I started laughing harder than I had before. He continued on in typical acid confusion, "Wait . . we're here, right? So the question is: Where are *they* in relation to where we are."

We broke down, unable to finish what we were attempting to discern. It's like that on strong acid. Every new encounter sets off a need to figure out the most insignificant matter like it was the key to understanding life's most basic mysteries. It allows for a semblance of connection between the simple and the abstract. The altered mind cannot process a problem from start to finish without getting caught up in everything in between.

Will and I had been caught by the trap. It could happen with anything. You could try to be figuring out if you had enough money to buy a soda or something and from there you'd be trying to grasp the whole biology of eat and drink, until you ended up convinced that all of human nature was just some alien conspiracy.

Will had just come to the conclusion that no one could ever really knew where anyone else was as long as they were out of his sight. I saw Kevin approaching as Will finished his final statement, "That's just the way it's gonna be!"

"What's all this about 'a new way'?" Kevin asked in his best imitation of a British screen accent. He was quoting one of our favorite movies and all three of us got the joke right away.

It was the first I'd seen of Kevin since he'd set sail on the wind of a second dose. His eyes looked like they were direct from storybook illustrations, being much too large for his head. I thought I saw them rotate in a retracted spiral, but that could've been due to my own warped perception.

Kevin was trying to talk to me but his words were getting lost in the lyrics of the songs and the scratching of the records. I was hit with a flash of fever as I tried to translate the movement of Kevin's lips into sensible language. I felt the need to get myself to the bathroom and wash the heat from my face. I excused myself and rose on unsteady legs, feeling the rush of tainted blood into the head.

I was losing my grip. It felt like my sanity was sealed off in some safe that hung from a height by a thin thread, like how the spine is held to the brain. In an instant that thin wire would snap, sending that safe sinking into the depths while my mind rose into a mist of uncertainty. The stark lighting in the bathroom did nothing to help.

It was a bit terrifying walking into all that brightness. The ceiling and the stained floor were revolving in alternation. The odor of shit and vomit came through and nauseated me. I ran my hand along the tile to guide me. I was light-headed and very unsteady.

I stood in front of the urinal but there wasn't anything happening. No flushing out of the system. It wouldn't work. I fucking hated when it wouldn't work. It was like my body was holding on to the drugs with all it had.

I stood staring at the words markered on the wall in

movable graffiti: "I AM THE WALRUS! COO-COO-CACHOO!" Man, I was taken aback with how appropriate those words were at the moment. I could've been the walrus or I could've been the carpenter. I could've been Christ or I could've been the crucifier. In my state, I couldn't be quite sure of anything.

I looked at the tiles and they were melting. In the mirror, my face was melting. The color of my shirt, reflected in the looking glass and refined through the tint of my glasses, was burning my eyes.

I ran my hands under the cold water pouring from the faucet. I cupped them in order to catch the droplets. I brought the water into position to splash my face and wash the fever away. As I stared into it, I thought I saw thousands of tiny brown insects swimming, but it was just a trick of the fluorescence.

I rinsed the bad effects out of my head. I let the water run down my face. There weren't any paper towels so I used toilet paper to dry off instead. I looked into the mirror for a parting glance. I saw every imperfection reflected back at me. It looked like I had a rash that was spreading at a quickening rate, and I thought to myself, "I am the Walrus!" Or at least I was making the transformation. I heard the voices returning in my head.

As I left the offending smell of the bathroom, the voices echoed in my head like a recording played at higher speed than need be. *"Coo-coo-cachoo, coo-coo-cachoo!"* screaming like ghosts from beyond the grave.

I scanned all the strange faces as I emerged from the blinding light. I felt like a soul that had been rejected from heaven and was cast back into the miseries of daily life. I was struck by how ugly everyone suddenly looked. My happy pill had gone the other way.

There was a panic eating away the inside of my belly, like I'd accidentally swallowed some radioactive protein and had to deal with the aftertaste. I staggered in a daze, unable to locate any of my friends. The place was congestive and I felt the walls of the club closing in on me like a python.

When I finally eyed the rest of the guys across the room it was like receiving an injection of pleasant pharmaceuticals. As soon as I was in their company, the good times would come back again.

I must have looked like hell, sweat pouring down my

face and all. I was out of breath and feeling worn out. Ryan looked up at me with concern.

"You alright, Brendon? You look like you've just seen a ghost."

I had. I'd seen my own pale and transparent ghost in the bathroom mirror. I just sort of nodded my head. "Yeah, I'll be okay. It's just hot in here, that's all."

"Well, take a seat then. We were just discussing the possibility of smoking some more weed in one of the stalls." I was watching Kevin as he talked. One glance was all it took to tell he was in a whole other world from the one I was in.

I took up one of the seats on a couch they'd secured. They were all speaking back and forth in such a flurry that I couldn't keep up. Besides Will, they were no longer on the same schedule as me. They'd accelerated into overdrive while I was stuck in the rewind.

For once in my short-lived life, the idea of smoking more weed didn't appeal to me. The last thing I needed was to increase the negative narcotic ailment in my body. Already, Taylor was rolling a joint for our consumption. I was feeling a little bit like a downer. They were all having so much fun. I wasn't gonna be the one to rain on their parade. I decided I would just leave before they smoked. Simple as that. I would get off my ass and proceed through the silver doors like it never happened.

"Let's do the dirty deed!" Taylor announced once the joint was all prepared. The rest all rose. Even Mikey got up out of his drug-induced sleep to follow the trail of would-be smoke.

They took a few steps before noticing that I was still nestled in the comfy cushions of the sofa. "What?" Taylor asked looking back at me. "Aren't you coming?"

"Naw, you guys go ahead. I think I might head on home."

Kevin started laughing and so did the rest. They thought I had to be putting them on. Go home? What, was I crazy? I could see them thinking it the minute I said it.

"You serious, Brendon?"

I felt Kevin's stare and I felt everyone else's. They stood towering over me in inquisition. Taylor had the same look he had earlier at school when he thought we'd snubbed him. Only before it hadn't appeared all twisted up into a modern sculpture like it did to me then. "You *got* to be kidding!"

I fixed my sight over on Will, knowing he was the only one on my level. Hoping *he* would at least understand the need to flee. Keeping my gaze on him, I told them all that I wasn't feeling tip-top.

I was in the trailing end of my peak, but peaking nonetheless. So when my would-be comforters crept closer they all appeared to be predatory birds. I crouched farther into the sunken sofa. I was having a really bad time of it. My mood was getting more erratic by the second. Their arm movements repeated themselves in the flailing motion of wings and I withdrew farther in.

They all kept asking if I was okay. I wanted to yell out that I'd be fine if they just got the fuck away and let me breathe. But they were only trying to help out and even in my state I was aware of it. They were too fucked up to notice they were scaring the shit out of me.

I started to say my partings to each in turn. They were still unsure if I was joking or not, but I ignored them. The scenery was getting grainy . . like the switch from analog to digital and I couldn't make the adjustment.

"You're not really fucking leaving, are you?" Kevin asked.

Yes! Yes! I really *was* fucking leaving! I didn't know why that was so terrifically hard for him and everyone else to understand. I stood, then made for the door, completely shrugging off Kevin.

He grabbed my arm and spun me around. "What's your problem?" he said, his face looking bitter and ugly.

"Weed ain't cool enough for you? You're too smart for that shit now?"

Kevin's tone told me he wasn't kidding around anymore. I could see the surge of unexplainable amounts of acid lingering behind his eyes. Staring deep into them, it didn't take much for me to tell him to fuck off.

He went for the dramatics, putting on like he was hurt only to show that he'd anticipated my remarks and that they didn't mean shit to him. Then it was Taylor chiming in, taking on the role of pushing Kevin along. "Maybe *we're* the ones who aren't cool enough," he said with a smile expanding across his face, impressed with his own simple wit. But he was a prick, so fuck all what he said.

"I'm bored." I yawned. I was through with this. It was old and tired and I was having trouble standing in an upright position.

"Oh, so sorry we couldn't entertain you more!" Kevin said, real sarcastic and leading up to what it was he really wanted to say to me. "Come on," he continued, "you're the clown here! Why don't you do one of your little acts and keep the party going since you're so fucking bored?"

I was all openmouthed and wide blue eyes. I hadn't expected the comments to get so close to the serious. Working through the mist that hid reason from my brain,

I stared Kevin down. I looked at the bend of his eyebrows and the distorted coloring of his face . . the television static in his gaze. I read his features as they twitched in a hallucinatory daze . . and then I saw the situation for what it was. There was a fucking mutiny going on and there weren't much I could do.

Ryan edged his words in between us. It was a deliberate and sudden movement and it shocked the hell out of me. His face was green with the reflections bouncing off his skin and his voice borrowed from some swampy rhythm. "Come on, let's just go and smoke, then you two can kiss and make up. Come on, Brendon."

Always the role of the peacemaker. Always calm and up for keeping an even tempo. But Ryan made the mistake of appealing to me, thinking I could defuse the situation by shrugging away and conceding. The Indian pipe trick wasn't gonna work this time. It was out of my hands. I couldn't. I couldn't go back into that bathroom with its face-changing mirrors and monster-under-the-bed memories for the sole purpose of further alienating my soul from my mind. Hell, I wasn't even sure I could walk, what with the crowd bending and swaying to block the way and the flickering lights deteriorating my sense of vision. Besides, I wasn't leading anymore. This was Kevin's battle to win or lose.

I looked over at him . . his face hidden in the shadows of the dark club. I knew something was coming, but had no idea what or how to brace for it. So I stood open and unblocked . . a stream of dancers softly twirling nearby. And I was scared all of a sudden. I was alone in the world, all of a sudden.

Kevin didn't hold anything back. He went at me in every way he knew how . . saying shit I hadn't believed he could even think. "You're a fucking asshole," was how he started off. "Blowing us off all night, hiding in corners, pouting like a damn baby!"

I stood mute like any good defendant. What the hell was I gonna say to that? He must have taken my lack of response as an invitation to continue because he got right back into it. "And why you always gotta talk shit about everyone behind their backs? Who the hell made you prince? You're just a skinny bitch!"

He paused and I rolled my eyes and felt faint. Confrontation was so tiresome while on acid. I was about to crack up laughing because I thought I saw a hidden smirk on Kevin's face. It was all a joke then? I wouldn't put it past him. But when he cleared his throat to begin again, I knew that was only wishful thinking.

Kevin got going at such a pace . . stringing together insults and obscenities like bullets in a wild Western. He was frothing and spitting and the like . . a tone taken from Nazi war films. He let his thick tongue run freely over the words, hungering to hurt me. I took them all in, *pervert*, *faggot*, *trashy piece of shit*. I wasn't sure where all of this was coming from, but Kevin was having a real go of it.

I was desperate. I didn't know what the hell he was talking about. And where the hell was Will in all this? I scanned around and back over my shoulder and saw Will staring into the flow of people, into his glass of water and down at his feet . . anywhere but at me.

The spiteful words just kept flooding in my direction, *sissy*, *pussy*, *deserter* and all the others. He was keeping time with the unshakable fury of the surrounding speakers. I was losing my balance, and once again Kevin resembled a vulturous bird . . his incredible wings creating a whirlwind to knock me down. The rush of people was heading right toward me . . their insane cackles mixing with the music and flushing the color from my skin. I was teetering, falling . . ring the bell and count to ten. It's a knockdown! It's a knockdown! But he kept railing me . . kept chirping and screaming and barking ugly orders. Jesus, throw the fucking towel! But there was still one more jab up his sleeve . . the good old low blow for a crowd pleaser.

"You never give a shit about anyone but yourself! You're no different from all those assholes you claim to hate .. greedy and egotistic. Think you're smarter and better-looking than the rest of us! Is that why you always trying to steal people's old girlfriends, to show you're better than the rest?"

I was stung. That was told in confidence and he knew it. There was no need to bring her into it. It was a sore subject with Ryan around and he fucking *knew* better. Now it was out in the open, and I was going to get shit for it for a long time because none of the guys really liked her. I was insecure about the whole thing as it was.

He'd gone too far over the edge. I could've hit Kevin right then .. taken a swing and just struck him in his flat fucking nose and laid down a pounding until the blood started to show. I let out a growl and meant to do it, but I could see that he was ready for the same. It's what he wanted and I wasn't gonna give him the satisfaction.

I looked over at Ryan and he looked away, pretending to be distracted. Taylor was standing there with a smile and looking stupid .. playing a game. With Will, it was like he wasn't even there and I felt like he wanted it that way.

"Let him go," Taylor was telling Kevin. "If he's gonna be a dick all night, why have him around?" It wasn't worth answering anything to Taylor's joining in. But Kevin? I wasn't gonna take his shit like a little child that's been kicked and taken down.

"You're a fucking animal," I told him. He didn't respond, just gave me that smug-ass look to let me know he'd won. I was on uneven legs and growing weaker by the second. Too many drugs and too much tension and everything goes to shit. The whole runaround and the rest was making me dizzy so that I wanted to just up and puke it. But I swallowed it back down, bitter in the back of my throat. I raised my thin hand and flashed Kevin the finger, saying, "A fucking, decaying animal and I can't stand the stink of you anymore."

I should've run then . . should've made a valiant exit, leaving it on a good insult. But my feet were failing and would not respond. The scraps between us had never gotten this far and I guess part of me was wanting to see Kevin react. I wanted to know for sure if he really had it in him.

When he did finally speak, he was screaming to be heard over the blaring beats of synthetic drums. No calm in him. No attempt to disguise his desire to tear me apart. "I'm the animal? Huh? I am?"

I didn't utter a sound. I was too exhausted to battle any longer. I stood with my head wavering, waiting for the attack to come . . wondering how far Kevin was willing to go over this nonsense . . debating what the limits might be because I no longer had any idea.

"Am I the one?" Kevin went on. "Am I the one who jerked off in the school bathroom? Am I the one who pissed my bed and laughed about it? Huh? Do I lie about all the girls I've slept with because I'm the only one who's still a *virgin*? Huh? You're a fucking predator! You should get your mom to take you back to the psycho doctor again! You're the fucking degenerate animal!"

They were all looking at me now, waiting to see what I would do. I felt the demons clawing away at my chest, ripping at sections of bone and blood and flesh . . trusted secrets torn from me and thrown back in messy clumps. I was stunned, betrayed, and stained. Christ, let the universe end.

My eyes were red and burning. All those stories, every one, Kevin had respected when I'd told him. Now he turned them all around . . reducing whole adventures into single sentences . . confessing things for me that I didn't want to confess. Knowing my fear of insanity and reinforcing it tenfold.

There was a madness gaining ground inside of me and a tightness in my jaw. I averted my eyes from Kevin, wondering if it was forever.

As calmly as I was capable of doing, I pulled Will aside. I told him I had to go. I had to get out of there. I needed him to understand. I needed for him to let me know I wasn't going absolutely crazy. But most of all, I needed him to speak up . . to say something in my defense.

Will just stood there, dull and mute. And when he nodded blankly, I almost cried. It wasn't what I needed from him then. Was he at all aware of what the hell was going on? Was he ever? The attack had been leveled against me and I had called in the backup, but he was a no-show. He kept up with the nod like some junky priest, incapable of verbal communication. He could've been nodding at anything . . at me, at Kevin, or at the flashing lights that were pulling me toward insanity.

The paranoia filtered in from all sides. Nothing was working according to the script my mind had written. The ceiling was slowly sinking in on me. People were passing by in waves and I couldn't concentrate on their faces.

When I couldn't deal any longer, I made swiftly for the exit without turning back. For a moment I thought they would come after me . . try to drag me kicking and screaming into the middle of all that confusion. But I wasn't sure they even cared anymore.

As I was getting farther away, I heard Will saying, "Let him go, he'll be alright!" But he had spoken too late for comfort.

Letting the cold night air rush against me, I tried hard to believe him.

I COULD TASTE THE FROST IN THE EARLY winter air. The release of each breath made the cold visible. It had taken several blocks of extensive effort to be able to think again. It had taken several slow blocks of one-foot-then-the-other procedure before all the faculties began to function. And it had taken at least that long for me to register the near-arctic wind in the air.

My hand was shaking as I held the cigarette between my thumb and forefinger. I took a deep pull even though my throat was hurting. I had smoked a lot more than normal during the last two days and I thought I could feel the cancer taking root as I walked with the light of the moon shining down upon me.

In my rush to escape, I had left my coat at the club.

My whole body was shivering in violent spasms from the cold or from the withdrawal symptoms . . possibly from the effect the fight left in me. I couldn't be sure which. Probably it was a combination of all three.

I was trying to digest the recent altercation . . playing the images over again in my head. Maybe I should've stayed and suffered through the wave of panic that had passed over me. But the more I thought on it, the more I was sure that I had done nothing wrong. No matter which direction I examined it from, the fault fell on Kevin. *Fuck him*, I thought. But with each step I felt an awful separation.

I walked without destination, without even considering where I was heading. I wasn't going home, that was for certain. I just walked farther and farther. The sound of my shoes hitting the cement was soothing. I was too afraid to stop. If I stopped moving then the steady sound would disappear and the wealth of silence would drive me insane.

Where was my fucking doll with white claws and the milk she needs? Where were the clouds I could eat? The water here was all polluted and brown. Where were the children with blue skin? Where the fuck was my dream, because this was when I fucking well needed it!

Being alone was like being unreal. I had no one to

bounce my thoughts off of. No relay of information to counter a horrible case of introspection. It was a feeling of needing friends around and not knowing if you still had any. Without them, I wasn't even sure I existed. The constant clamoring of my shoes was all I had to reassure me.

I stood under a flickering streetlight, admiring its precise timing. On then off. On then off. In the moments between, I was able to disappear. That is the sensation I thought of when I thought about the bright side of suicide. It must be like turning off what you didn't want to see anymore. And at that moment, it was myself that I didn't want to see anymore. Myself and the ridiculous costume it was dressed in.

Each time the electric fuse clicked, I had to squint. The light would strike the fabric of my shirt and sting my tired eyes. My hit was showing hardly any sign of fading. It was always that way whenever I wanted it to end.

I kept my eyes on my stomach as the shirt stretched against it. There was a bloating inside, like I was pregnant with a baby growing, only the baby was swimming in flames instead of amniotic fluids. Every time the light would return from absence, I half expected to see signs of growing rounder in the belly until I'd give birth by retching fire from my mouth. I wanted to rip off the thin shirt I was wearing and poke around to make it come faster. I wanted that horrible thing out of me.

I buckled over onto the concrete, the thick pink contents leaking from my stomach in heaves. The yellow lenses of my glasses cracked as they hit the ground. I watched as the tiny fragments came to rest in the contents of my vomit. I wiped my chin with the back of my hand.

Sitting there under that off-and-on-again light, staring into my own intestinal liquid, was about the first time I ever remembered feeling cold. I mean the kind of cold that dissolves the bones and reaches into the soul. I sat there, hands tucking my knees into my chest and drowning in the cold. I wondered to myself about when it had happened. When did I start growing old? When did life start being something you had to work at and not something that just is?

Things were falling apart all around . . the buildings with their fractured ceilings and the sidewalk with its uneven pavement . . broken bottles and the fragments they left behind . . personalities that I used to know and own. It seemed like the entire city was fashioned after a disposable dream and I was cursed with awareness.

I tried to stop my mind from thinking, but it wouldn't respond to my commands. The acid had me stuck on the bad side. I looked up at the vacant windows staring back at me and wished it all would end. Wished I could fall asleep and not wake up again.

I felt the wind kick in and turned away. I felt the crying creep in. But I held onto it, held the sour tears tucked inside like my knees were tucked under my chin. I had already given enough of myself to those unforgiving streets and I'd be damned if I was gonna give anything more.

I sniffed it all back up like a little girl with a scraped elbow who's trying to be brave. I hadn't heard the approaching footsteps until they were right on top of me. I hoped it would be Will or someone else I knew because even though I couldn't be near anyone, I didn't quite want to be alone either.

I looked up and turned my face to the corner where the noise was coming from. My vision was bleary, either from the acid or from the tears that maybe I'd only imagined that I'd held back. I wiped my eyes and when my sight didn't improve any, I knew the acid was the culprit.

The street was bathed in an orange haze like a thick, gaseous fog had rolled in from Outer Space. I couldn't penetrate it fully, but I could see enough to know that it wasn't Will who was coming my way. It was a stranger. Tall with a long-legged stride that seemed out of proportion with the world around.

He must have seen me 'cause he stopped a good ten feet away. I felt his watching eyes rest their sight on me. It burned with an invading quality. "Mind your own fuckin' business!" I wanted to yell, but he was much bigger than me and I was in no state to defend myself.

It scared me the way that man stood there because in the city you learn to be scared of every man that is unfamiliar and takes an interest in you. My stomach was turning over in a nervous sort of way. I released the tight grip I had on my legs and let them stretch out in front of me. Then I stood, very slowly, because the sickness wasn't gone yet.

I started walking real calm-like. I couldn't let that man know I was worried, couldn't let him know I was under the influence because they're both invitations for assault, both signs to let him know I was free for the taking. So I started walking like nothing was wrong. Only it was hard because I heard those other steps fall in behind.

I had a plan brewing. I'd walk at an even pace to the

end of the block then take off running in whatever direction was nearest. I could see the shadow moving in. I didn't think I could make it to the corner but I did. I increased the rate of my legs to superhuman speed, running until I couldn't feel my feet touching pavement anymore.

I wasn't at all surprised when I heard the quickening of steps trailing behind me. It made me push harder until I felt the ache of fire throughout the skeleton of my body. I knew if I could outrun him then I'd win.

The old man ran out of steam quick. He must have been a junkie-mugger looking for a fix, else he would have lasted longer. He gave chase only for about two blocks or so before giving up. I wasn't worth it, I guess. He'd move on to other prey that would be less determined to escape.

Even after I was safe, I couldn't stop running. My legs were stuck in their reflex motion and my racing brain was unable to pull them out of it. I kept thinking of different nightmares of pain and how much I hated people for being so revolting.

It wasn't like I was afraid that guy would shoot me or

kill me. No, Philly isn't the kind of city where you'd get murdered. It's more of the old-fashioned kind of thug mentality. I was more likely to get stabbed, or jumped with baseball bats, or sold for money so some sick fiend could get his high. And it was thoughts of this kind that kept me running. It's thoughts like these that can keep you running your whole life if you don't say fuck it and get on with living.

It wasn't until I found myself in the old warehouse district over by Spring Garden that I finally paused to catch my wind. I freed a much needed cigarette from my depleted pack and lit it. I saw an ease of mind in the glowing at the tip. And as it burned down I tried to forget why I had sprinted there to begin with.

Standing in that empty part of town, I had the feeling that I had died once that night. My vision cut through the walls of brick, the cement, and the nonsense. I looked closely at the rusted hinges that held weathered doors together by the splinters. I examined the rooftops as the sky came to lay its weight upon them. From left to right, I swept the expanse of ruins . . factories now fit only for ghosts to make their homes in.

I stood perfectly still, admiring the symmetry of erosion and realized how fleeting life could be sometimes. The old, sad music was cueing up in my head . . the kind of tune an orchestra plays when the princess of the ballet has died. But it wasn't a princess that died, it was my own sense of purpose. I was wandering around like a peasant on the very same streets I usually strolled with an attitude like I was the king of 'em. But the guy I was the day before wasn't there with me and I was struggling to breathe at the realization.

I wanted someone to come along and hold me. Not like the way a dirty bum trying to touch on me would, but the way a mother holds her small child. I wanted some gentle woman to take me to her breast the way this woman did in a Steinbeck novel I had read. I wanted to be nursed back into the years when nothing but imaginary monsters terrified me. But there weren't no one going to walk by. It was just a futile wish like the ones I'd had as a kid, always wishing that I would grow up to be a medieval wizard or a knight riding off to slay loathsome dragons.

I don't know when I stopped hoping for dreams to come true, but I did. Hope just goes the way of the drug during the coming down, leaving me dry and tired. The idea of pretending no longer appealed to me.

The internal monologue was running in my head and I had trouble following it. I had no control over what it said. If I couldn't shut it off, then I thought all it said would be true, like it wasn't me talking but rather some dictator of fate. It was like a word virus and I had no cure for it. It spouted out all my insecurities and laid them bare. It told me that I would die crazy and there wasn't no religion gonna save me.

I let my back lean against the brick wall, soaking in all the pollution that littered the area around me. I looked over at a sprinkler attachment that was leaking into a puddle on the sidewalk. Drip, drip, drop. Drip, drip, drop. I let the pattern regulate my thoughts. I let the freezing wind remove away all feeling. Then, ever so quiet, I started to sing . . allowing the years to slip off like so much dirt that needed washing. And the sound of my voice and the childish song it sang made me smile for the first time in hours as I listened.

"London Bridge is falling down,
falling down, falling down.
London Bridge is falling down, my fair lady."

THEY SAY IN THE MEDICAL JOURNALS that if a person drops acid more than three times in his life then he's legally insane. Well, I had passed that point a long time ago, and the voices in my head seemed to confirm the myth. But if it was true and I was insane, I was gonna enjoy it. I wasn't gonna be one of those crazies that hid away in the cellar afraid of everything. Hell, I was gonna shove it in the world's face and make them smell it.

I took up walking in those near-dawn hours with just a little taken off my usual swagger. I made my way up Market Street, passing glances into the store windows to make sure I still had a reflection. And each time I saw it, I ended up giving myself the finger.

Then I'd laugh because it was funny. It was funny

how I'd thought my mission in life was to offend everybody on some level, just to make them think. I mean to really think hard about their own sorry lives. But when I saw my polyester-clad, puke-stained self prancing by in the fancy glass, I realized I'd never thought about my own sorry life.

I used to think that I could pass through life in a fantasy, that if I did enough drugs and dreamed hard enough then I could leave this hellish world on a permanent psychedelic holiday. I could become a piper with a patchwork jacket made of tweed, piping a flute through the fields of wheat in some Kansas of my mind's invention. All the buildings, the advertisements trying to sell me things, they would all drop away and I'd be free. But the reality of it was that I was stuck right here whether I liked it or not.

This plastic culture abounds. It keeps everything sealed neatly inside for sterility's sake. There was no escape. No breaking through the barrier to the other side where people danced in a pastel haze. I had been striving for that fairy tale, but it was all bullshit and illusion. The whole routine was worn out and tired.

I wiped away the fever with the back of my hand. I felt like a fool who watches the world spin around in orbit. I thought I was so fucking clever all the time, always so creative, so spontaneous. But what the hell was I *really* doing? Now, I was beginning to understand it. The world wasn't going to dissolve and leave me alone in a coloring book setting. And if I couldn't flee it, the least I could do was fight against it.

I tried to spit on the rare cars that would come my way. I even walked in front of this one beat-up old junker to force it to stop. The young woman behind the wheel went half out of her mind at the sight of me. I must have looked deranged and crazy. It was stupid but I couldn't stop. I raised my arms over my head with wrists bent slightly. My eyes bugged out of my head and I screamed straight into her window, straight into her bloodshot eyes. I didn't scream any words or nothing. I just screamed noise like a territorial bird warning intruders. I starting pounding my fists on the hood of her car and let loose in that manner. My lack of all control frightened me. The woman shifted into reverse but I hung on, still howling at the top of my lungs. As she swerved to go around, I spit and spit into the windshield blocking her face.

As the auto pulled away, revving its rusted engine, I frantically looked for a bottle or something to throw its way. "FUCK YOU!" I screamed until the car was out of reach, until my voice traveled its way into the ears of good old Billy Penn way atop City Hall.

If the guys could've seen me then in the middle of my psychotic episode, they would've laughed, laughing until they fell flat on their asses. But for once it wasn't for their sake that I did it. I did it because that's how I felt. I wanted to send the whole miserable world to hell and I needed to show it. I wanted to prove to the world that it was mine and that I still owned it. I wanted most of all, though, to prove it to myself because I no longer felt it.

I was walking with a fucking hop in my step because it was freezing. With the acid in remission I had lost the little protection from the cold that I had. And even though the day was coming, it wasn't warming up none.

The old, rich ladies were out with the rise of the sun. Wearing their fur coats and walking their wimpy dogs and averting their eyes from me as I came up the block approaching.

I looked like something out of a worn-out commercial, like the cameras had stopped rolling but I just kept with the part I was playing. I saw this one elderly couple leaving their upper-class apartment building and it made me think about everything I was sure that I would never have. I would never get that place with a view or a woman who I could grow old with.

As they got nearer, I dipped into the cover of the bus stop to take a piss. Hell, if it was alright for the dogs, then it was alright for me. I hoped that the old couple would see the stream or at least hear the whistle of it as it hit the street. I wanted them to realize what they had. To let them know it was a great thing to find happiness among so much filth.

I looked back to see them shaking their heads, and I smiled and said good morning. Fuck 'em. If they couldn't get the message then they weren't worth the effort.

I was still gonna lead the rats from this fucking town no matter. Drop the flute! That season is over. I would scream, high-pitched and dramatic, if that's what it would take. Take them out with piss! Take them out with rude gestures and a fucking bloody fist! Didn't matter by whatever. I'd be the piper if I was ever gonna be shit. Watch them flee in flocks by way of airlines and foreign cars and other means of transportation. I could march the broad streets with a fucking skip and leave the dust to drift behind me. Make this shit town fit for blue people and clouds that I could eat. Made fit for princes with dirty cheeks and dressed in rags. Made fit for animals that scurry and mice that sing. I'd make this world fit for my dream if it wasn't going to come to me.

I got to thinking that no one in this lousy city was worth the cost of all their possessions. None of them knew what it meant to be part of the living. Drive the whole fucking lot of 'em out and live in peace! Live alone among all this shit.

That's when I started to think on the dying again. It would be so easy and so pleasing. I would just let the winter wash over me and bring me into the place where there were no more thoughts to trouble me. The last great escape. I was done gambling, done betting on a ship that would never come in. I would cash in my chips while I was ahead. I didn't want to suffer the growing old, didn't want to wait until my memory went. It was all so tiresome. I would just go out in a blaze of glory before the parasites of sadness got at me and made me bitter. After all, that's the American way: take your own life before everything else takes it from you.

I WANDERED ON IN AIMLESS STRIDE. Looking for the doll with white claws. Looking for the underpass to heaven. Looking for some fucking sign that I was still living.

I found myself walking west . . the way of the dead. Counting the streets increasing in number. That's how Philly's laid out. The streets don't count up, they count further toward death.

Black smoke slugged out from the exhausts as the cars rolled through the intersections and out of my sight. The sun was shining and it was an awful day. I needed an angel. I needed a fix of stimulants. I needed warmth and the dull glow of TV. I needed sleep. I needed to be awake. I needed the smell of green grass and dirt. I needed seashells. I needed coffee and a fucking newspaper. I needed gasoline. And we all need oil. I needed a fucking haircut because it was clouding my vision. I needed something because I could feel my stomach start aching.

I wanted wings. I wanted cigarettes and nobility. A double-breasted suit with the elegance of a torn wedding dress. I wanted a change of scenery and a backdrop of theatrical set pieces. I wanted communism for the upper classes. I wanted to be the life of every party. I wanted only to be anonymous in a big city. I didn't care much for luxury. Christ! Why does everything require thinking?

I could feel the ghosts in my spine. Kicking and whining. I couldn't keep it up much longer. Had to be somewhere. Had to do something. It was all getting too depressing. Had to take things back to the beginning.

I headed to the park and toward the promise of recovery. Had to detox. It was the only place to be on a Saturday in autumn after you've been beaten by a strong dosage. I had to clear my head of the shit that was filtering in. Had to shake the ghosts from pulling me under. The risk of drowning being very much present.

Onward to the square! To the park! The place of revolutions and uprisings and general discontent. From there, I could set things right. Snipe out the rats with positive energy and such. I just had to find some first.

Absorb it from the flowers and the trees and grow strong by association. Breathe it in. Steal it from children. Steal it from the wind. Steal it from wherever, but just get it inside me.

When I got closer, I realized I was still looking for the dream. Still reaching for the things that weren't going to happen. The demons were laughing in my head and clawing at my chest and they were winning. I didn't know what was real anymore or what was imaginary. Drifting with the waves. I didn't know the snakes from the birds. I didn't even know myself from the rest of the world.

Once I got to Rittenhouse Park, I went and sat on the same bench I had sat on two nights before when searching for the instant of purity that comes with the last rays of the sun's reign. Thinking back on it, it all seemed like so much glamorized bullshit. Just another foolish romantic notion like thinking that one person could change the world just by treating life a certain way.

I sat there shivering through the dawning hours, watching as early-to-rise families made their way into the park for a stroll in those four square blocks of nature. I hated how the little children would look and see the longing on my face. I hated even more the way my bedraggled sight frightened them away. All I needed was for one of them to come up and ask me in those tiny voices of theirs if I wanted to play. I would've jumped at the chance, too.

I waited, but it didn't happen and I felt like my heart had been broken. The ache was there in my womb again. Everything circling back around to boredom and emptiness again. Even the leaves were stale and unchanging. Everything stable. Everything normal. Just as fucking tedious as it ever was.

Swallowing was hard because I couldn't bring up any of the spit. Morning was coming on like a bad memory. It was the belly of the sun that rose, bright and magnifying, but there were still only stars that shone in my head. It was exactly the kind of mythic emotion Will would understand.

I swung around, looking and expecting to see him perched dimly beside me. But it was only the wind that blew up and covered the bench . . only a barren patch of the cityscape. The shivers ran deep through all the channels. I was past expiration . . the drugs passed through the body in phases of the veins. I turned my attention to the gravel and the squirrels and the things within my vision.

A little boy was being hurried along by his mother who was in some sort of adult rush. He stomped and pouted and pulled to hold her back so he could go at his own exploratory pace. The toddler's protest made me smile because there was no way he could've won. In a fit, the boy discarded a stuffed animal he was carrying. When I shouted to get the mother's attention, she purposefully ignored me. Christ, you can't even do a good deed without being looked down upon. But for the tyke's sake I got off my ass and went to pick it up for him.

I took a winding diagonal route and got there too late. The mom had pulled her son too far away from me and I didn't have the energy to shout. I bent down and reached for the toy, anyway. It was a cuddly kind of bear with a round nose that served no purpose. I looked into its fixed expression and felt the old, sad feeling welling up again. I clutched it to me . . cradled it like some gift from the past.

I sat right there on the hard ground, holding that toddler toy like a treasure uncovered from the bottom of the sea. That bear stared up at me like a relic from my own childhood days, trying to communicate. I had hoped it was telling me that those days weren't gone forever, they were just lost somewhere in all the growing. But when I really listened, I knew that wasn't what the bear was saying. It was simply saying good-bye.

Nevertheless, I kept the bear in my possession even if it did depress me. I took it back with me to my perch on the city bench. It carried with it the sour smell of an infant who had vanished and would never come back to claim it.

The poor bear had died then. The boy had made it all that it was. I mean, hell, it lived inside his little head. Now that he had gone, the bear was nothing. Stiff and without a personality. Even a fucking teddy bear needs his friends to live off of. Like everyone else, he's only made up of the people around him.

I decided to give it a proper funeral with all the pomp and ceremony it deserved. Pink streamers and the low tune of trumpets playing and all that. I thought I might even cry when I scooped dirt over him, but I couldn't be sure if I had any tears left in me.

Before I got around to all that though, I wanted to take a nap. I was tired, tired like the trees that sagged with the sway of the breeze. I tucked the little bear under my arm to keep him from the cold that I was feeling. I put my head lightly against the flaking paint of the wood I had been sitting on.

I had come here with a purpose, but I knew I was too terrified to deal with it. I came here with the hopes of finding my guardian angel. I couldn't wait any longer for her to find me. That's the process, isn't it? The angel comes to those in need? Well, none ever came to me, so I was going to bring it on myself to claim my own.

I came here because this is where she goes to get away from the grime and the clutter. This is where she comes to "get a little green in my life." And I needed to see her. I wanted Melissa to see me like this . . to see who I was falling into becoming. I came wishing she would be here . . fucking well knew she would be here. But it should've been before now. She should've been here before now! My head was telling me to go look . . to move my ass and go see her. But I was so tired. I needed some rest. I needed the brief comfort of unconsciousness.

I STUMBLED OUT OF SLEEP like a zombie all jacked up on hallucinogens. Caught in between stages and such. I felt distant from myself and from the lost hours of the night. Bruised and shattered, waiting for all the king's horses and all the armored soldiers to glue the fragments into place. I felt like a phantom, like I had only watched from a distance as things had happened. I needed something concrete to bring me back, to put me together.

Two days ago, I was somebody. At least I was impersonating somebody. But a bad trip and one forgets all that. A strange combination, toxin and truth serum. Poison and medicine. Like that ancient kid . . flying level with the sun only to be burned and drowned because of it. But the game wasn't over, I knew that much. I could still fucking win. Still had one more life and one more quarter for the arcade.

I had the shoulders slumped over . . had the walk of a stylized junkie from some old novel . . had the hair all blown wild. Loitering first class and taking in the glances. Here I am! Here I am! You can't catch me!

Then I stopped, left in an awkward stance. She was narcotic. I saw her walking . . steps like a child actress . . a born star and the toss of her hair like 70s television, done with flair for flair's sake . . apparently unconcerned with thoughts outside her head. If Melissa was an angel, then I certainly was the messenger cast from warmer climates.

The way she moved you could tell she was in touch with the pace of the world. Hip to all its twists and angles and way fucking superior to them. She had it all figured out, while I sifted through the muck for anything to grasp onto.

I went toward her. I'd meet her halfway. I'd make the move . . make the effort . . try for some connection. I was fragile. I stood in her path in sacrifice. I needed her calm reality. Her acceptance of me.

She walked with the sun to her back, casting a long shadow and putting me in the horrid spotlight. She crept closer, not noticing me. Reducing the distance between us and growing larger. When my sore eyes adjusted to the glare of the day's brightness, they came to settle upon green eyes and my own shaggy reflection.

"Jesus Christ, Brendon! What the hell happened to you? Are you alright?"

I tried hard to speak, but it was like I was trapped in air that's thin and tough to breathe in.

Taking me by the waist, Melissa led me over to the grass and sat me down. I felt the bundle of clothing sweep over me as she covered me with the feminine scent and sealed-in warmth of her coat. The motion of the hand that moved through my hair was like the touch of a spirit drawing me ashore after a long sailing on the sea of crazy.

Lying down, I stared into her eyes for a long time. It felt like days and nights passed with me just sitting there. No exchange of words. No intrusion of sound. Nothing happening in terms of action, but it wasn't boring. There was something magical in it for me. I couldn't explain what. I didn't want to explain. Didn't want to lose touch with these feelings. All the concern in her, all the pity, it succeeded in doing what nothing else that night had. It brought the tears into my eyes where they found the grip wasn't so tight anymore.

Reaching up, I took her free hand into both of mine.

It was warm and stung my own. The expression on her face remained calm. Her cheeks were glowing like a child's and her eyes were like glass in the sun. I near melted away and my weakness wasn't stemming from her beauty but from her compassion.

"You're such a little boy," she said. The first person to smile at me the whole day. And she was right. I had the old kindergarten instincts again . . holding hands with a girl during the Pledge of Allegiance while the teacher smiled because she knew there was something good and American in all that. That's the way Melissa could make me feel. There's something so real, so natural, so god-damn free about it that's so beyond articulation. That's her secret. That's what made her unlike anyone I had ever met.

I looked deep into her eyes and sobbed out the whole sorry story from start to finish. And Melissa listened. She listened to me ramble on even though she was freezing because her coat was covering my stiff, frozen body. I told her how I had spent the night in some horrible nightmare, only it had been real enough for me to get sick in. I explained the way my mind drifted once the acid mixed in. How I was different from what she might imagine me to be . . from what I had imagined myself to be. I told her about the toy she found me holding and what it meant to be abandoned by all your friends. And when I was done, those eyes didn't scorn me as I had expected. None of the "what the hell were you think-ing" . . the "playing with fire's gonna burn you" business. None of the horror or the shock. None of the policeman questioning. Her eyes were clear and hid nothing. They passed no judgment. They only grew more charitable and lovely.

I took a long look at myself and felt embarrassed. My hands and clothes stunk of nicotine and vomit. There was a long moment of silence in which only the nearby dogs were talking. "What the hell am I doing?" I finally asked her.

She didn't have an easy answer and neither did I. Lifting my head from her lap, I sat up and she put her arms around me while she thought. Her gaze wandered from place to place and back again in search of words that were worth saying. I could sense her passing over cautions and warning because that's not her style. She didn't presume the right to tell other people the way to live. She was above that sort of behavior even if she did tend to know the better of two choices.

After a pause, her voice came through clear and steady. She started off with a once-upon-a-time tale about a boy who put on like he had it all . . who sauntered the streets and came off like a right bastard to strangers and to himself. But the boy inside wasn't mud and shit and all things crazy as far as she could see. Sure some of that was there because it always is, but it's one and the same with the good. And when she finished, it was poetry and eloquence and pretty things I needed to hear.

She talked me down . . nullifying my fears and my doubts. Letting me see how stupid I was . . how carried away I'd gotten as tends to happen when the highs and the drugs exceed pleasure and become motivations . . bring you to the extremes of fun and leave you down and bored and disinterested in the things that suck. But I guess you gotta be part of some of the things that suck if you are going to ever enjoy the highs again.

I had listened the whole time to every word. It felt like there'd been a wound rotting in my chest, exposing weak bones and empty space. Now it was healing up . . slowly and evenly and with expert care. Better than drugs that don't work in the long run.

"It's only living," she said to me. I took a deep breath, tasting the scent of trees and cars, studying on the things Melissa had said. I was feeling good, a bit like my old self again.

"It's only living," I repeated softly as I smiled.

"Yep! And you look all the worse for it," she told me.

I stole another glance at the shabby figure I cut and started to laugh. Sniffing from the cold I'd recently caught, I said, "I guess you're right. I do kinda look like something someone stepped in, don't I?"

Then I added, "But in a cute way, right?" because I thought she was just a little too eager to agree. After giving me a once-over, she said that she guessed it was kinda cute, but only because my shirt was made of polyester.

We were both laughing and lightening the mood. Then Melissa asked me if I wanted to go to her place and she would make me some soup. She lived right around there, it wasn't that far to walk. Fucking soup! I just sat there shaking my head. I really got a kick out of life sometimes, the way it threw you a curve, low and away, when you were looking for that fastball to belt you in head.

I didn't go with her. I didn't want to end up messing with a dream that seemed too good to be true. Why force it? Maybe it was my old fears again, but I didn't think so. I was just too wasted to remain coherent. Melissa and I had spent the most perfect moment together, and I didn't want her impression to change by having me pass out in a bowl of chicken noodle.

"Okay then, but you should at least go home,

Brendon." I told her I would and she offered to escort me. I said she had done enough just by saving my life and I didn't want to trouble her. I said I would take a taxi so she wouldn't have my death on her conscience.

That made her smile, and her smile made me happy for the first time in what felt like years. Then I started laughing, I mean really kicking back having a blast of it. It was funny how I could barely bring myself to say hello to this girl in the many months I'd had a crush on her, but once I was beaten down by the world, I was suddenly able to bawl out my most private thoughts. Man, I couldn't believe the way life worked sometimes!

I wanted to tell her I loved her, and for the first time in my life I knew that it wasn't only my imagination. I really did love her. But I held back, again not wanting to spoil the moment. Instead, I looked at the wave of her strawberry hair that hung along the sides of her triangular face. I studied the shape of her mouth and every line her body made silhouetted against the crumbling city in the background, never wanting to forget it. And in my head, I had already memorized every soul-saving word she'd said to me.

I opened my mouth to speak but had trouble finding the words. Melissa encouraged them with her warm smile. I stumbled in a stutter. "I . . I," I said, trying desperately to recover. "Melissa," I finally got out, "thank you. Thanks for everything. I mean it."

She reached out and held my hand. "You did the same for me once. Brendon, you're really sweet, better than most. I couldn't let you lose that. I'd be losing someone special," she said and that was all she needed to say.

When she got up to leave, I gave her back her coat. I watched as her legs strode away and I almost rushed to catch up with them. But as I was about to stand and follow, Melissa turned back and waved. It was so sincere, so final, that I needed nothing more. I let her go . . my eyes tracing the path of every step as she went.

AS I LEFT THE PARK THAT SATURDAY, I felt like I had been born a second time. I no longer looked at all the people with disdain. It wasn't that I had become some lover of the human race overnight or anything. It was just that I now knew that they didn't matter. All that counted was the way I saw myself, not the way others saw it for me.

I took the last cigarette from my pack and smoked it. I walked those rundown streets with renewed purpose . . with a little teddy bear poking out from my breast shirt pocket. My turn to play the savior. I was gonna bring that little guy back to life along with me.

I was feeling good, like there were acoustic instruments and symphonies playing for only me to listen to. High volume. Fucking great stereophonics and the drummers were hitting the right rhythm. Notes painting canvasses in my head with colors I'd never envisioned before.

I found that the fields of Kansas exist among the Philly concrete. And I felt completely free for the first time in my life. And I remembered thinking that it was true what they said, you had to go through hell to get to the other side where it's greener.

I thought I might go over to Ryan's and wake up everyone to see if they wanted to get something to eat. Then I decided against it. I'd see them all soon enough, but later. I didn't need company. I didn't need to play my bit for them right now. Eventually, but not until I let all the sickness blow over. Which it would. Hell, Kevin might even stop by tonight with a peace offering and fuck it, I would hang in the park with him. Brothers are like that. But for the moment, there was pleasure to be found in my own company. There had been enough doubt and worrying there, it was time to look in at the good.

Maybe I would get on a bus and head out of town. I could use a break from the city . . the closed walls and closed sky. Land stretched out for miles, no need to be confined. It was wide open. Might always be. But why chance it? Go when you felt it, that's my attitude.

Maybe I'd go out to the country and go fishing. Dip my ankles in the stream and let the sun borrow color from my polyester. Hike through the woods like a boy pretending he's Tom Sawyer or Huck Finn or William Shatner. Maybe smoke a joint and get in touch with nature. Maybe stay sober and then see where I could find excitement. And then, when I got back, I might ring Melissa and see if she wanted to go on a picnic.

Wherever I was going, I decided to go by foot. I would be careless. I would fast. Or I'd eat if I fucking well felt like it. Didn't matter. Still doesn't. I'd go north the way of Santa Claus and falling stars. Head through the slums and row homes and the dealers peddling crack and penny dreams. The symphony still going strong in my head. The pitter-patter of rats trailing behind me. And me walking like I fucking knew I was the man.

Cal's got this thing about fire. It's nothing big at first, just lighting matches, watching them burn, enjoying the calming effects of the flame. It helps him cope with life.

Then he meets Abby, and things start to get out of control. He lets her get close, and she winds him up, playing with him until he thinks he might lose his mind. Suddenly the matches aren't enough.

So Cal comes up with another plan. A bigger plan.

Nothing will ever touch him again. . . .

KEROSENE

by Chris Wooding

THE BEDROOM WAS EMPTY, the sunlight of the late autumn afternoon a pale wash across the crazy-paving pattern of the duvet. A bookshelf stood next to the bed, cluttered with comics, graphic novels, markers, sable brushes, jars full of dirty water, and other assorted odds and ends.

The walls and ceiling were black, but they were painted with a variety of bright cartoons, all following the same motif: clocks. Grandfather clocks, alarm clocks (digital and analog), watches, cuckoo clocks, and more. Some had faces, some were melting in the style of Dalí, and some were blank, with no hands or numerals. Some smiled, some leered, some had teeth, some winked. They floated in a starfield, and a few of them had been captured as they drifted behind another, giving the paintings a curious three-dimensional perspective.

On the wall above the bed hung a clay effigy of a tribal wolf-mask, its flat snout snarling emptily. A wardrobe and a chest of drawers leaned against the other wall, groaning under the weight of the junk that had accumulated on top of them. In the center of the room was a mobile of little wooden baby angels painted brightly with cutesy faces beaming, or with their expressions scrunched up with the effort of blowing their tiny horns. A poster of Larisa Oleynik as Alex Mack was positioned in pride of place opposite the window. A stereo system rested on the floor beside an untidy stack of CDs.

The room was silent.

Then, dimly, there was the sound of a key rattling in a lock downstairs. The latch thudded back, and the front door opened, whining on its hinges. There was a slam as it was closed behind the newcomer, then the sound of footsteps hurrying up the stairs. The door to the bedroom was flung open, and a boy of about sixteen entered, ignoring the "BIO-HAZARD" warning sign on the outside. He threw the door closed behind him and slumped down heavily on the edge of the red-and-white bedspread, his head in his hands, breathing hard.

It was a small, thin figure that sat there for a long while, unmoving. His baggy jeans were scuffed and flecked with bright paint. He wore a heavy-knit black sweater that dwarfed his bony shoulders, and a blue T-shirt beneath. His brown hair stuck out everywhere, an uncontrollable ragtag mop.

"*SHIT!*" he screamed suddenly, his voice sounding raw and high. He sprang off his bed and kicked his chest of drawers hard, sending rolled-up drawings and badges toppling off the edge. Unsatisfied, he laid into it viciously, planting the sole of his battered Converse on it again and again. Next he turned his wrath on the blank face of his wardrobe. He swung a punch into it, his fist driven by a desperate need to hit something, *anything*, to vent the frustration that seared through his veins.

The pain brought him back to his senses. He near broke his knuckles with that first punch, so just to spite himself he threw another one with the same hand. At the last moment, he couldn't help pulling the force out of it. His body was instinctively trying to stop him from harming himself. But it still connected, hard, and the blaze of agony that exploded in his hand almost made him pass out.

His good hand clamped around his wrist, he sat back down on the bed, his teeth clenched while he fought back the urge to cry, ashamed of the tears that pricked at his eyes. The pain in his hand eventually began to subside; the turmoil in his head did not.

It had been one of *those* days. God, it was so *humiliating*. One of those days when he couldn't look anyone in the eye, when he had walked along the road to his house with his attention fixed firmly on the ground in front of his feet, shuffling meekly along so as not to draw attention to himself.

He had been doing alright all day. And then just on the

last stretch, the walk home from the shops, it had all come crashing down on him. He had seen a tall guy with a skinhead wearing tight black jeans and cherry-red Doc Martens, walking along the other side of the road. Mildly interested, he was looking over at him when the guy turned round and met his eye. He had experienced a sudden, unpleasant thrill at being caught staring, and turned his eyes away.

But a moment later, the skinhead had whistled at him, a short, sharp *wheep* through pursed lips. He looked back, feeling a terrified nausea creep into his belly, and the skinhead had flicked him the finger, saying: "You wanna photo, mate? Last longer."

He felt it sweep over him like a cloak. Hot blood flushed into his cheeks, prickling heat across his face and the nape of his neck. His throat tightened at the sides, his heart began to pound, he was sweating, he felt sick. He turned away from the skinhead, looking down, wishing he could disappear. The skinhead didn't hassle him anymore. But the damage was done.

The remainder of the journey was a nightmare. Everyone on the street seemed to be looking at him. It was as if his affliction marked him out, making everyone stare at him. Like some kind of freak. He was conscious of walking fast, but he couldn't help it. He had to get off the street, away from the piercing glares of the passersby.

When he had finally gained the safety of his house, self-disgust had flooded through him. *Why?* Why so afraid?

Afraid? No. *Shy.*

He snorted, smiling bitterly. A sweet word. When people thought of shy, it was always kind of cute. Nice. Coy girls in floral dresses, wide-eyed cartoon squirrels. Not a crippling, awful sensation that made your tongue too thick to speak and locked up your brain. But that was what it meant to him. And it unmanned him, made him pathetic and weak and *ashamed.*

Trembling, he got up and walked unsteadily to the drawers that he had battered seconds earlier. The clocks swam around him in the starfield on the walls. With his good hand, he brought out a box of Swan Vesta matches. Crossing the room, he closed the thick blue curtains, shutting out the dull light, plunging himself into darkness.

He sat back down on the bed and pulled out a match. Slowly, speeding up as he got to the end, he drew it along the sandpaper. It sparked first try, flaring white as the phosphorus head caught, then settling to a steady yellow flame. He watched it, fascinated. Shadows flickered deep on his face in the light of the match. The heat of it was comfort to him. He stared into the heart of the flame, and felt some of the frustration drain out of him. There was peace there, at least.

He let the match burn down, only blowing it out when the pain in his fingertips became too much to bear. He sat there in the darkness for a while, feeling better. Flame was such a calming thing. Just a little match, and he felt okay again.

It was enough. For now.

PUSH YOU ARE HERE.

PURE SUNSHINE BRIAN JAMES

cut
Patricia McCormick

KEROSENE
chris wooding

you
remind
me of
you
a poetry memoir
by eireann corrigan

IN STORES NOW

****

BE A PUSH AUTHOR. WRITE NOW.

Enter the PUSH Novel Contest for a chance to
get your novel published. You don't have to
have written the whole thing — just sample
chapters and an outline. For full details, check
out the contest area on ***www.thisispush.com***

****

ALEX + MICHAEL
♡forever